Singles Cruise

Singles Cruise

Jacalyn Boggs

SINGLES CRUISE

Published by Erendi Publishing

www.erendi.com

Cover design and interior layout by Erendi Publishing.

First paperback edition: 2025

ISBN: 978-1-950903-30-6

Printed in the United States of America

SINGLES CRUISE

© 2025 Jacalyn Boggs

Published by Erendi Publishing

www.erendi.com

This is a work of fiction. Names, characters, places, and events are either the product of the author's imagination or are used fictitiously. Any resemblance to actual persons, living or dead, businesses, or locales is entirely coincidental.

Cover design and interior layout by Erendi Publishing.

First paperback edition: 2025

ISBN: 978-1-950903-30-6

Printed in the United States of America

Singles Cruise

Jacalyn Boggs

Dedication:

For anyone who's ever packed more emotional baggage than actual luggage—this one's for you.

For the ones still figuring it out—your faith, your future, your place in the world.

Whether you're healing from heartbreak, learning to love yourself, or just here for the shuffleboard and dessert buffets, know this:

You are worthy of love, laughter, grace, and second chances. (And thirds. And fifths. Especially if cake is involved.)

Here's to believing again—in love, in miracles, in fresh starts, and in the absolutely wild idea that your best days may still be ahead.

Chapter 1

"What's this?" Grace looked from the thick envelope in front of her to the three women sharing her table at Alex's House.

One motioned for her to open it while the other two grinned. "Call it whatever you want—just open it!"

"Paige, what did you girls cook up now?" Grace eyed the envelope, which looked plain enough. One of her friends slid a butter knife across the table. With a sigh, Grace picked it up, sliced open the flap, and pulled out the contents.

"CruiseLady's LDS Singles at Sea," she read aloud, her brow furrowing as she dropped the brochure onto the table. "A singles cruise? I told y'all—over and over—I've sworn off men."

"Oh, don't be silly," Paige said, pointing at the brochure. "It'll be fun!"

"There is no way I'm parading my lily-white legs in a swimsuit trying to pick up a man. I'm definitely not doing it while surrounded by young gals in bikinis. I'm not that desperate. And... and... I'm just not that desperate!"

"We're not saying you're desperate," Dawn countered. "Just that you need a vacation. Besides, this is a Mormon cruise. Good little LDS girls don't show their belly buttons, remember?"

Paige nodded. "Yeah, and just think of the adventure! A trip out of the country? You'll have so much fun!"

"A cruise? I can't afford that, and I definitely can't afford the time off." Grace tried not to look at the tropical pictures on the brochure's cover. She really didn't want to admit how wonderful a vacation sounded.

"You deserve an adventure," Hillary stated, folding her arms. "You don't have to afford it. If you'd just look a little further in the brochure instead of being so negative, you'd see."

"What did y'all do now?" With a groan, Grace flipped through the pages. Nestled in the middle she found both a cruise ticket and round-trip airfare from Raleigh to Baltimore.

"What? I can't... I don't... what is this?" she stammered, stunned.

"It's a gift, so accept it, Grace. You've been saying you need a break for months, and we agree!" Hillary clapped her hands, smiling wide.

"Paige found the CruiseLady's site and told us about it," Dawn added. "We decided it'd be perfect for you. Honestly, we're jealous you're going. But we knew you'd never spend your money on it." She waved a stern finger in Grace's direction.

"We know you, Grace," Paige chimed in. "Aaron would need a new pair of tennies or something. We wanted to do this for you, our husbands supported it, and we even talked to your ex! He said he'd be glad to keep y'all's son."

Hillary giggled. "If Seth hadn't agreed, we'd have done it for you and sent the missionaries to his house daily just to torture him."

Paige grinned. "Hey, maybe we'll do that anyway. It'll be fun. The Elders need a challenge, right?" The other two nodded enthusiastically. "This bunch thinks they can convert every lost soul in the Triangle. Meeting Seth Jackson will keep them hopping."

Grace burst out laughing. "Paige, you're horrible—but I love you for it." She sobered, glancing at each of her dear friends. "But I can't miss work. I still have to pay the bills. I'm sorry, I can't accept this. Please, please tell me the tickets are refundable."

"Grace, it's called PTO," Hillary said firmly. "You have it. A week's worth, and it kicks in a month before the cruise. You won't lose any pay, you've got babysitting covered, and you'll have some spending money. You are going."

Her eyes flashed. "We don't give a Lamanite's loincloth if you meet a man or not! You need a vacation, and this fits the bill. Now say, 'Thank you, my bestest friends in the mortal world,' and order something before the waitress kicks us out of her section."

Hillary sat back with a smug smile as the other two gave her high fives.

Grace glared at her three friends for a moment, then closed her eyes with a long sigh. When she opened them, tears shimmered in her eyes.

"Thank you, my bestest friends in the mortal world. I don't know what I'd do without you."

She paused, trying to compose herself, then added with a faint smile, "I still don't know why the waitress hasn't brought our food yet. We eat the same thing every month. Geez. And someone answer this—since y'all seem to have the rest of my life planned—what the heck am I going to wear?"

Dawn reached into her purse and handed Grace a gift certificate to the mall with a wink.

"I was waiting for you to ask that."

They flagged down the waitress, placed their usual orders, and turned their attention back to the brochure, voices buzzing with excitement about the cruise.

Chapter 2

"Think about it, Spence—a week away from it all. No work, no phone calls, no emails. Just us and the open sea. Add that to the fact that we'd get to walk on the same land as... Nephi. C'mon. You can't resist that. You *know* you want to." McKay gave Spence a nudge in the ribs, clearly enjoying the chance to tease him about his obsession with all things Nephi.

Spence cleared his throat and absentmindedly fingered his Angel Moroni tie tack—a gift from his youngest sister. A flutter stirred in his stomach at the thought of standing on what might be considered "holy land." His first year of Seminary had been focused on the Book of Mormon, and his teacher had sparked a lifelong interest in the ancient places mentioned in the text.

His dream of serving a mission in South America had ended the day his call letter arrived, sending him instead to Australia. He didn't regret the experience—it had changed his life—but he'd spent years praying to teach the gospel in the lands where Nephi had walked. How could he say no to this, at least without considering it?

"Okay, Mick. Give me the brochure. I'll think about it."

"That's my boy." McKay's far-off look made it clear he was already daydreaming about the young single women waiting aboard the ship for an RM ready to pick his eternal mate.

Spence took the brochure and eyed the glossy photo of a luxury cruise ship splashed across the front. Arching an eyebrow, he dropped onto their futon and propped his feet on the beat-up footlocker they used as a coffee table, careful to avoid the various church magazines strewn across it.

"*Singles at Sea?* What the heck?" He growled and smacked McKay with the brochure. "You said this was an educational tour, not some LDS meat market. Forget it. Not interested. Have fun—and tell the future Sister Grant I'll be sure to warn her about all your annoying habits before the wedding."

He dropped the brochure in disgust, letting it land on top of the latest Conference Report.

"Cuz, I can't go alone. Think how *desperate* that'd look to the ladies. Besides, you don't have to go for the women. You're ancient as the ruins in their eyes. Leave the ladies to me. *You* go for... Nephi. Nephiiiiii..." McKay waved his arm dramatically over his head as he dragged out the name.

Spence stood, crossed the room, and punched his cousin in the arm. "I'm not ancient. I'm not even close. I'm not even forty yet."

He stepped into the cramped kitchen, grabbed a plastic Taco Bell cup from the dish drainer, and filled it from the tap.

"Besides, I've been married. It's not like I'm a perpetual bachelor or anything. But that last conference you dragged me to—those kids looked so young and innocent I could *feel* my gray hairs shining." He shuddered. "The girl I danced with told me she was only two weeks old when the Challenger exploded. That's what I get for bringing up NASA."

Returning to the futon, he slumped down again. McKay stood in the middle of the room, looking like he was still mentally assembling his next Nephi-themed argument.

Spence sighed and stared into his cup of water. There was no point in fighting—McKay would wear him down eventually.

"Okay, Mick. I'll go. But no matchmaking. No 'poor old cousin Spence' nonsense. No bragging about our pioneer heritage. I'm not looking for a wife—been there, done that, got the wedding ring back. I'm going for the tours. The divorce has only been final for a little over six months, and honestly, I'm just not into all of that."

"Spencer Fielding Olsen, you are my favorite cousin ever. And we've got a *lot* of cousins." McKay dropped onto the couch next to him, grinning. "We'll have a blast, you'll see. Or at least *I* will... You'll have a, uh, an *educational experience*."

He ducked to avoid a playful smack to the head. "You do your boring tour stuff, and I'll pick up the hotties in tankinis."

Chapter 3

A few weeks later, Grace opened the door to her small two-bedroom apartment.

"Come on inside, Aaron."

As she lugged in a bag of groceries, Aaron dodged past her and ran straight to the toy box. She watched wearily as he pulled out a dump truck and began driving it in wide arcs around the living room.

"Boys— all play and no work," she murmured with a quiet laugh, grinning as he swerved around her feet. She made her way into the kitchen, put away the groceries, and popped a frozen pizza into the oven.

After setting the timer, she stepped into the small dining room where a little table for two sat beside her desk and computer. She flicked the machine on just as Aaron zoomed by again. This time, she scooped him up mid-run and hugged him tight.

"Whatcha doing, Aaron?"

"I'm working to clear out dirt to make room for houses!" the little boy declared proudly. "I have to work hard. After I get done, I'm gonna build us the biggest, nicest house! It's gonna have the bestest backyard and a treehouse!"

Grace blinked in astonishment. He was going to build her a house?

"What are we going to do with this house?" she asked gently.

"Well, I'm seven now, so I need a huge room and a bunk bed! And we can get a dog because the house is gonna have a fence! A big dog! Like Lassie or something!" His eyes lit up with sparkling innocence. "Wouldn't that be the bestest?"

Grace smiled and ruffled his sandy, curly locks. "That would be the bestest. Especially since you're building it."

"My room is gonna be decorated with dinosaurs! Rawwwwwr!" Aaron pulled away and started stomping around the room like a T-Rex, much to her amusement.

She raised an eyebrow and asked in mock seriousness, "Dinosaurs, huh? Aren't you going to get scared being surrounded by all those dinos when it's time to sleep? Wouldn't you rather do cowboys?"

"I'm not scared, Mommy! I'm big and brave. I'm not six anymore—I'm all grown up! Dinosaurs don't scare me!" He puffed out his chest and marched off to his bedroom. A few moments later, Grace heard him digging through his toy box and playing with his plastic dinosaurs.

She turned back to her computer, shaking her head at the brave declarations of little boys. As it booted up, her gaze landed on the cruise pamphlet resting beside the monitor.

She picked it up and ran her fingers across the glossy page before opening her browser. Her friends didn't call her the Internet Queen for nothing. In minutes, she'd pulled up destination info, cruise line details, and about fifty testimonials from past attendees claiming the trip was "great and relaxing." She even found a full photo journal posted on someone's personal blog.

She tried to ignore the testimonials of "true love found" while sailing the high seas.

With a click of the mouse, she maximized the photo journal. Picture after picture filled the screen: glorious beaches, bright blue skies, ancient ruins, and modestly dressed sunbathers lounging on the deck of an ocean liner. Grace smiled.

Maybe this wouldn't be so bad after all.

She leaned back in her chair, then reached for a notebook to jot down ideas for possible photos. The photographic opportunities thrilled her, and she added a few camera-cleaning supplies to her growing shopping list.

Still, despite the excitement, Grace couldn't help the worry creeping in. The last Single Adult activity she attended had felt more like a high school dance than anything else. She'd found herself hit on by all the freshly returned missionaries.

Not that she had anything against RMs—but Grace wasn't interested in dating someone who'd been home from the field for a week.

Every one of those bright-eyed boys had backed away the moment they found out she was divorced and had a school-aged child. She just couldn't compete with all the perky eighteen-year-old girls dancing their carefree hearts out. Not that she wanted to. She remembered being that young—and didn't want to think about how long ago that had been.

Sure, she worked hard, and her divorce had been final for almost a year and a half. But when she looked into Aaron's eyes, she knew it was all worth it.

Even dealing with her ex—something that could bring her to tears faster than watching Sleepless in Seattle—was worth it to have Aaron.

Grace wouldn't trade her life for anything in the world.

Chapter 4

What do you mean, you're getting married?"

Spence slumped into the recliner, clutching the phone with white knuckles while running his free hand through his hair.

"Julie, you've only known this guy maybe two months..."

McKay stared at him, making various frantic hand gestures.

"I know it's none of my business anymore what you do," Spence continued, "but Julie, come on. Think about what you're doing. Think about what we did. It was a mistake... no, not the entire thing, but the rush. I... I just think you need to pray about this."

The color drained from Spence's face. McKay stopped gesturing and mouthed, Are you okay?

"I see," Spence said into the receiver, ignoring his cousin. "Well, good luck then. No, I'm not mad. Like you said, it's none of my business anymore. Julie, I've gotta go. Mick and I are going to the gym." With that abrupt end, he hung up the phone and stood.

McKay jumped in immediately. "What'd she want? What'd she say that upset you so bad? Cuz, you don't look so hot. Maybe we should skip the gym—"

Spence turned and stalked to the bathroom, slamming the door behind him. A few minutes later, he reemerged smelling of toothpaste and mouthwash.

"Let's go," he growled, already heading toward the door.

The ride to the Richmond YMCA was quiet. In the locker room, Spence changed into his swimsuit without a word and headed straight for the pool. Without so much as a glance at his cousin, he dropped into the water and began swimming laps.

Though eight years apart in age, the cousins had always shared a love of swimming. Spence had once made it to nationals and was mid-interview with a U.S. Olympic recruiter when his mission call arrived. His mother called with the news right in the middle of the meeting. McKay, meanwhile, had delayed his own mission for a few months, debating how far he wanted to go with competitive swimming. After being unexpectedly cut from the U.S. Team trials, he served a mission in Chile.

Ten laps later, Spence emerged from the water and clung to the pool's edge, breathing hard. His voice came out shaky. "She's pregnant, Mick."

"Son of a brick. You're joking?" McKay hoisted himself up onto the concrete beside him.

"Years... I wanted to have a child with her, but she said she wasn't ready. Long years, McKay. I understood waiting while I was in school. But I dreamed of our children—waiting for us to bring them into this world. And she said, 'Soon, Spence. Soon.' Always an excuse. After school, it was 'Wait till you get your practice established.' Then, 'Maybe next year.' Always 'maybe next year.'

"And then—boom! She's gone." He tried to snap his wet fingers but gave up. His voice rose into a bitter imitation. "She 'just thought she should call and tell me herself.' Don't I just feel peachy?"

He shoved himself out of the pool and started toward the door marked Men's Showers. McKay followed, scrambling for something to say.

"Forget her, Spence. Think about the cruise next week. We'll find you a woman who'll be more than happy to give you ten of the finest Olsen babies this family's seen in years. I'll make it my mission—and you know how good I am at missions," McKay added with a proud grin, remembering the fifty-seven souls he'd helped bring into the fold in Chile.

Spence turned abruptly, causing McKay to bump into him.

"Mick, I am not looking for another wife. In fact, being single for the rest of my life is starting to sound awfully good right now. I'm going on this cruise with you, cousin, and I'm going to immerse myself in ruins and history. The ancient past. Not mine. That's all."

He met McKay's gaze, daring him to object. When McKay remained silent, Spence turned and continued walking.

"Yeah... keep thinking that, Spencer," McKay muttered to himself as he watched his cousin disappear through the door. "Story goes, that's just what Grandpa said right before he met Grams in Jerusalem."

He rubbed his hands together with glee. Fine, he thought. Maybe my cousin doesn't want to get married. But if McKay could help him meet a nice new female friend? That would be a start. Maybe it would even help mend a broken heart.

He understood where Spence was coming from. His cousin had taken the divorce hard. Less than a year ago, his supposed eternal companion told him to "take eternity and the Church and stuff it," before walking out the door to "go live life." That wasn't the sort of future any young man envisions.

Now, news of pregnancy and a wedding—in that order?

McKay hated seeing Spence suffer. But he also knew something else.

Spence was an Olsen—and Olsens? Olsens thrive on happily ever after.

It was in the genes.

Chapter 5

Grace held up her new swimsuit for Paige to see. "What do you think?"

The floral one-piece came with a matching sarong and a beach towel in a similar color. Thanks to a generous gift card and an end-of-season sale, the outfit had been a steal.

"Oh, *dahling*, it is *glorious*," Paige drawled dramatically. She seemed more interested in the pile of clothes strewn across Grace's bed. Picking up a frumpy pair of overalls, she let out a sigh of pure dismay.

"What's your problem?" Grace asked, though she already suspected Paige's frustration.

"Look, I *know* you aren't interested in meeting any of the hotties on the ship—but please. You can still look pretty. You don't need to hide behind these clothes. You're single, you're gorgeous. If you've got it... flaunt it!" Paige flung an arm overhead and struck a ridiculous pose.

"You're crazy. I'm going for comfort. I don't care what I look like." Grace snatched the overalls back and stuffed them into her suitcase. As she turned toward her closet, Paige retrieved the overalls from the suitcase, dropped them on the floor, and quietly kicked them under the bed—where three other pairs had already met the same fate.

"Grace, take this dress. Definitely. And these shoes. But those frayed cut-offs? They're not invited. Guys aside, you're going to be on a big boat in exotic locations. You at least want to look *halfway* decent. Think about your pictures! You'd never forgive yourself if your scrapbook pages had you dressed like you were cleaning toilets five minutes before all the action."

Grace paused. Paige had a point. She'd already sketched out some scrapbook layouts for the trip. Her goal was to have the whole adventure chronicled and tucked away by the end of the month.

"I suppose... you're right," she said reluctantly.

Paige did a small victory dance, then flicked the shorts across the room to land on a chair. She neatly packed the dress and shoes into the suitcase.

She looked up just in time to see Grace holding a precarious stack of books and magazines. "What is *all* that?"

"Something to do on the boat." Grace looked at her collection, unable to decide which to bring. Between working full time and raising Aaron, her TBR list had grown out of control.

"Are you planning to hole up in your room with those things?" Paige narrowed her eyes.

"Um... no?" Grace offered, though it wasn't convincing.

"That's it. You—out to the living room. I'll finish packing. You are *not* going to look frumpy. You *will* look fab. You are going to have FUN. You are going to NOT take a bunch of stuff and be antisocial. You WILL go to the activities AND the tours!"

Paige grabbed the books and magazines, tossed them onto the bed, and physically ushered Grace out of the room. With a dramatic slam, the door closed—and locked.

"Hey! This is *my* vacation! Let me back in!" Grace banged on the door and rattled the knob.

"Not likely. I'm in charge now—and you are going to have fun!"

Paige quickly packed Grace's cutest summer outfits and tossed in the suntan lotion for good measure. As a kindness, she selected two magazines and one very short book from the discarded pile. Zipping the suitcase, she carried it to the bedroom door—just as the doorbell rang.

From inside, she heard Grace muttering and making her way to the door. Ever nosey, Paige cracked the bedroom door and peeked through.

Grace had just reached the sofa when she kicked a toy train piece and nearly toppled. Letting out a short cry of pain, she hopped the rest of the way to the door, wiping away a tear.

"Hello, Grace."

She froze. Seth.

Her ex.

Of course he'd show up when she looked—and felt—her worst. Her face flushed as she carefully placed her sore foot on the ground.

"Uh, hi. Thanks for taking Aaron this week, Seth," she murmured, eyes downcast. She limped into the living room to grab a small suitcase emblazoned with a bright cartoon character.

"Aaron, your father's here!" she called.

Aaron bolted down the hallway and straight into his father's arms, clutching a massive Lego creation.

"Hey, sport! What did you do—use every Lego in the house?"

"It's a boat! Like Mommy's!" Aaron giggled.

Seth's eyes flicked to Grace. She busied herself with inspecting the suitcase, trying not to meet his gaze. He plastered on a smile and turned back to their son.

"That's... great. Let's go. We're picking up Becka and getting ice cream!"

Aaron cheered. Grace handed over the suitcase and knelt for a long hug.

"Be good for your father. I love you forever."

"I'll love you for always," Aaron replied—a line from the book they'd read so many times it lived in their hearts.

Once the door closed, Grace sagged against it.

Paige appeared with the suitcase.

"So... who's Becka?"

"I dunno. Some new girl. Who can keep track?" Grace hated how dejected she sounded. Seth always seemed to have someone new. Meanwhile, she'd had three lousy dates since their divorce—and that had been over a year ago.

Paige gave her a sympathetic look. "Oh honey. It's okay. Just remember—tomorrow, you're boarding that big boat for a week of sun, sea, and scriptures! Don't worry about Seth."

"You're right. I just..." Grace blinked back tears.

"Come on." Paige grabbed her hand. "I'm putting your suitcase in the car. Then I'm taking you out for milkshakes and cheese fries or something indulgent. We'll talk about your trip and have fun."

Grace offered a weak smile. "I can't do that. I'll never fit in my swimsuit tomorrow!"

"Oh please. You're going to eat on the cruise, too. Come on. You and me. Giant milkshake. Maybe a movie. How about a pedicure so your toes are cute in your sandals?"

Grace sighed. "I probably won't be much fun. I'm just so tired all of a sudden."

"Then you'll fall asleep during the movie. Like we haven't done that before." Paige winked. "You're staying at my place tonight anyway so I can drive you to the airport. Come on—it'll be like a slumber party."

Chapter 6

"Look at the size of that thing!" McKay stared up at the cruise ship, wide-eyed. "Spence, you seeing this?"

Spencer, however, wasn't looking at the ship at all.

"Spence? You okay?"

"What? Did you say something?" Spence's absentminded tone earned a dramatic shake of McKay's head.

"Earth to Spence! We're on vacation. Join the party!" McKay shifted his duffel bag and grabbed his cousin by the shirtsleeves. "Come on, man."

"I'm sorry, McKay. I just can't stop thinking about—"

"Don't say it. I know what you're thinking about." McKay held up a finger. "New rule: No saying her name, no talking about her, and definitely no thinking about her. Once we step on that boat, she does not exist. Got it?"

Spence gave a tired nod as McKay practically shoved him up the ramp.

Thankfully, it was still early and the boarding line was short. Armed with their room assignments and a map of the ship, the cousins set off to find their cabin.

"This place is massive," McKay muttered. "Think we'll ever find our room?"

"Dunno. We might already be lost," Spence replied, still not quite present.

"Did you finally realize where we are? This is magnificent!"

"All right, all right," Spence relented. "Luxury vacation might be just what I needed."

McKay's stomach growled. "I just hope we can find our way back. To the food."

Spence chuckled. "Shazaam, McKay. Ever think about anything besides your gut?"

McKay grinned. "Yup. Girls! So let's ditch our stuff and go find both."

Rolling his eyes, Spencer muttered, "Girls and food and food and girls. You're so predictable. No wonder your mother's gone grey."

"Hey now! I'm a delightful son. Never caused her a moment of grief!"

Spence arched a brow. "Sure. You're as innocent as the day you were born."

"Well, I am!" McKay huffed and turned back to the door numbers. "Hey, Spence! Found it!"

McKay dropped his bag and fumbled with the key. The door swung open to reveal a surprisingly plush room.

"Check it out. Our own luxury liner cabin. This'll be a great story for the next mission reunion."

"Whoa... nice." Spence stepped inside and dropped his bag onto an overstuffed chair. McKay chucked his duffel onto a bed and flopped down dramatically.

"Ahhh. Almost as good as home."

"Yeah right. You won't spend any time here. You'll be too busy hitting on every poor girl who made the mistake of booking this cruise."

Spence began unpacking, neatly folding and placing clothes into drawers. McKay watched in disbelief.

"You're actually unpacking? Baaah! I'm gonna go see who else is here."

"You know other people?"

"Nope. But I figure there have to be girls coming. And who better to greet them than us?" McKay flashed a perfect grin.

"There'll be plenty of time for you to flirt. We've got a whole week."

"Never too early to stake a claim, Spence. I'm sure I'm not the only RM on board looking for eternal love. The honeys love us RMs."

Spence shook his head, amused and horrified. "Good thing you're ready to swoop in as their knight in shining armor."

McKay winked. "Exactly. I'm off to rescue some damsels—with luggage!"

McKay wandered down the corridor, hoping someone had left a door open for spontaneous conversation. Turning a corner, he nearly plowed into a young woman struggling with a massive suitcase. He narrowly avoided crashing into her—but not the suitcase.

"Oh my heck, I'm so sorry!" she exclaimed in a lilting Southern accent. "Are you okay?"

"I'm fine," McKay said quickly, trying to look cool despite hugging the wall. "Need a hand?"

The suitcase was practically the size of a small piano. He grabbed it with ease.

"My friend packed it. I don't think I'll use half of it!" she said, cheeks pink. "I can't even find my room. I think I've been going in circles for twenty minutes."

McKay took her key card and smiled. "Lucky you. You're just down the hall from me. I'll help you out."

He led the way, dragging the overstuffed case and wondering if it was full of bricks. At her door, he heaved the bag inside.

"Thanks," she said. "This ship is just... huge."

"No problem. My cousin and I are just down the hall. I'm McKay. My cousin's Spence."

She smiled. "Grace. Nice to meet you."

"Well, Grace, I'll leave you to unpack. See you around." He gave her a charming nod and left.

Chapter 7

Grace waved as McKay left. She unzipped her bag and stared at the sheer amount of stuff Paige had managed to cram into one suitcase. Still standing over it, unsure where to begin, the door opened a few minutes later.

She looked up as a young, blonde woman all but skipped into the room.

"Well hi! I guess you're my roommate!" The girl beamed with a model-perfect grin and bounced toward Grace. "I'm Meghan—but you can call me Megs. All my friends do!"

"Um, hi Meghan... er, Megs." Grace already felt overwhelmed by the bubbly stranger.

"Oh my heck! I'm so excited to be here! Are you?" Megs didn't seem the least bit fazed by Grace's hesitation. She pulled in her coordinated luggage and immediately began unpacking—talking the entire time.

"My golly, I couldn't believe this cruise when I saw the pamphlet on the Singles Ward bulletin board. I had to go. I mean—what better way to spend a vacay? Sun, water, tan, and a whole boatload of eligible bachelors! I figure if I work it right, I'll totally come back to BYU with a handsome RM on my arm. Can you imagine? A whole boat of single LDS guys! And how romantic would it be to meet my future husband on a cruise? Of course, he has to be a return missionary from a foreign-speaking mission. Then our honeymoon could be to the country where he served. How dreamy is that?"

She finally stopped and looked at Grace, clearly expecting a response.

"Um... really dreamy?" Grace offered, unsure what else to say.

"Oh my wow! Are you okay? You look a little pale. Maybe you should sit down!" Megs' cheerful tone shifted to one of concern.

Grace did feel a little dizzy. Maybe she should get some air—or maybe she just needed to escape. Listening to Megs talk about fairy tale romances was not helping. The last thing Grace wanted was to crush this girl's dreams, but marriage sounded like the least appealing thing in the world right now.

"I'm fine, just tired," she said. "Maybe I'll go for a walk. Get some fresh air or something."

"Oh, let me go with you! I mean, we can't have you passing out in some hallway. Although—how romantic would that be? You could totally faint, and some gorgeous RM would catch you, and then your eyes would meet and—bam! —insta-love! Then in two months, you'd be sealed in the Temple and have the cutest story ever!"

Grace's stomach turned. "You know... I'll probably be fine. I'll just go up to the upper deck and get some air. You can stay here, really. I don't want to inconvenience you."

She made for the door, hoping for a clean getaway.

No such luck.

"Oh just wait," Megs said, grabbing her hand. "Here—sit. I'll get you some water. Then we'll go up together. We're roommates this week, and we should totally be there for each other!"

Grace reluctantly sat. Megs filled a glass from the bathroom tap and returned triumphantly.

"I'm sorry it's just tap water, but we'll find something better once we're up on deck!"

"Um, thank you." Grace sipped politely, her heart sinking. Megs seemed like the opposite of relaxing. Could she really keep this energy level up all week?

Megs chattered on. "So I'm from Baltimore. I'm a sophomore at the Y. My younger brother just got his mission call to Denmark—so cool, right? My dad and older brother served in Germany. I might go after next year, unless I get married first. I mean, my husband and I could go on a couple's mission when we're older!"

She paused, suddenly aware she'd been monopolizing the conversation. "Oh my gosh—I'm so rude! I don't even know anything about you! What year are you in college? Tell me about your family!"

Grace sighed. "I'm Grace. I'm not in college. I work at a photo lab... near Raleigh." Some days she felt so old and tired, it was flattering to be mistaken for a student.

"Wow, a photo lab? That's so cool! Do you have, like, a darkroom and everything?"

"No, it's all digital now. I do whatever's needed, but I make most of the product samples."

"Product samples? Like what?"

"Well, I love scrapbooking, so I usually make sample photo books. We sell some basic supplies, so I also design scrapbook pages for the store display. Most people get their stuff from the craft store next door, though."

"That's adorable! You must love Enrichment nights! Do you work on the Enrichment board?"

"No. I don't really have a calling right now. I was just released as Primary chorister a few months ago. It's been a little stressful, so the Bishop hasn't called me to anything new."

"Primary? Why not go to the Singles Ward?" Megs tilted her head. "They're so much fun! And everyone's single. No worrying about falling for a guy who turns out to be married!"

"Um... I don't go to the Singles Ward." Grace could feel it coming and braced herself.

"Why ever not? I mean, we're only single once. You should totally enjoy it!"

Grace's face flushed. She knew Megs didn't mean anything hurtful—but this part was always hard.

"I can't go to a Singles Ward. I have a son. So I need a ward with Primary."

Megs' jaw dropped.

Well, Grace thought. That's one way to render her speechless.

"I—I'm sorry," Megs stammered. "I didn't know."

"It's okay. You didn't know." Grace stood, set the glass on the nightstand, and walked to the door. "I think I'll take that walk now."

Thankfully, Megs was still too stunned to follow.

Chapter 8

Grace leaned over the railing and stared at the shoreline. With the smell of the sea in her nose and the wind in her hair, she felt herself relaxing. Her friends were right. She needed this.

Many people were still boarding with their luggage and trying to find their quarters, so Grace found herself staring at the sea with just her thoughts for company. Thirsty, she made her way to get a virgin strawberry daiquiri from the nearby bar.

She took a sip of the refreshing beverage and scanned the deck, hoping to find a chair to lie in and relax. Okay, I could get used to this. Peace, quiet, warm weather, and a cold drink. Heaven.

Distracted, Grace tripped over the leg of a nearby chair. She caught herself, with both hands, and watched open-mouthed as her drink went flying and landed...right on a man with a white tee shirt on and a swimsuit, sitting on a nearby deck chair leafing through vacation pamphlets.

"Oh, Shazam! Oh no! I'm so sorry! Here, let me help you." Grace grabbed the napkin wrapped around her drink, oblivious that it had been soaked through, and started dabbing it on his shirtfront, pushing icy chunks into his chest.

"Cold! That's cold!" Spence grabbed her hand and pulled it away.

"Oh! oh, I'm sorry! I didn't... oh shoot a monkey, I'm such a klutz! Wait! I bet I have something in my bag that will help that stain." Grace limped to sit down and unzipped her small bag. "Ack! Darn that Paige! She told me I had to bring this tiny pocketbook instead of my big one... hold on! I remember seeing some stain wipes in my monster suitcase. C'mon!" Grace grabbed Spence's hand, pulled him up, and raced towards her cabin. "Really, I'm so incredibly sorry. If we can't get the stain out, I will pay for your shirt. I'm just so embarrassed."

Spence followed Grace in silence and lost in several stages of shock, mostly because he could not get a word in edgewise or get his hand free. She kept rambling about how sorry she was. The surprise of the drink spilling on him, the jolt of the cold seeping through to his chest, then the reaction of this beautiful woman with the soft, small hands, was enough to keep him quiet. He snapped out of his daze when he realized they were on the same hallway as his cabin. Confused he gaped at McKay, who opened the door just as Grace dragged Spence by.

"Whoa, Spence, nice shirt. Hey, where are you guys going?" McKay followed as Grace barreled down the hall muttering under her breath about her . She stopped at her door and let go of Spence's hand to look for her key.

"Hey, I remember you! You're the girl with the overloaded suitcase...Patience...Faith..." McKay wracked his brain for her name.

"Grace. Yeah. Where'd you come from?" Grace answered, just noticing McKay had joined them.

"Well the long story is from my mother. The short one is from my room, I saw you two when I came out." McKay sent Spence a weird look.

"Oh." Grace opened the door and pulled Spence in. "It's in here. Somewhere. Give me a minute." She began to root through her suitcase to look for the stain wipes.

"Hi, Grace! Wow, looks like you brought the party to our room! Go girl! Hi! I'm Megs. And you are?" Megs bubbled, holding out her hand.

"Cold. Uh I mean, my name's Spence." Spence shook her hand as he watched Grace digging around in a large, over packed suitcase.

"I'm McKay Grant. Wonderful to meet you, Megs. We are in a room just up the hall. If there's ever anything you need…" McKay flashed a million dollar smile.

"Absolutely. McKay. Nice name. Very nice. Where are you from? Do you go to the Y?" Megs smiled, totally in her element flirting with guys.

"You really don't waste time do ya? I like it!" McKay winked and grinned at Megs and draped his arm around her shoulder companionly.

Grace popped up with a hand over her head in triumph. "Found it! Okay, you, strip." She pointed to Spence.

"Grace!" Megs exclaimed.

"Woohoo! My kind of woman!" McKay laughed, and nudged his cousin with his free arm.

"Umm, shouldn't we introduce ourselves first? Or at least let me buy you dinner?" Spence asked and grinned awkwardly.

Grace turned several shades of red and took a deep breath. So much for a graceful first impression. "Okay, let's try this again. It'd be easier to treat the stain if you'd take the shirt off. Not to mention more comfortable than wearing it, I'm sure. Oh, and I'm Grace the Klutz Jackson."

"Spence the Cold Olsen," he said with a grin as he pulled the wet t-shirt over his head. "It's nice to meet you, finally. And seriously—don't stress about the shirt. It's not a big deal. Accidents happen."

Chapter 9

Grace let out a breath she didn't realize she'd been holding. Maybe this cruise wouldn't be so bad after all.

Spence stood in the center of the room, still shirtless, while Grace tried not to stare—and Megs audibly failed.

Oh wow, Grace thought. Paige might be right—maybe she was overdue for an adventure.

"Hey Cuz, I'll go get you another shirt, 'kay? Megs, want to walk with me?" McKay saw the appreciative looks passing between Spence and Grace, and he thought a few minutes alone might prove interesting. Not to mention, he'd get to know Megs a little better and free up some space in the cramped cabin.

"Sure! Grace, we'll be back in a flash!" Megs tossed over her shoulder in her bubbly way as they left, the door swinging shut behind them.

"I'm really sorry again. I tripped. I'm always doing stuff like that," Grace said, for what must have felt like the hundredth time.

"Really, Grace, it's no biggie. Are you alright? You got bumped around a bit." Spence glanced down at her feet, noticing her pastel pink toenails.

"Yeah, it's fine. My feet are used to getting banged up. I'm forever stepping on train pieces and Legos at home." Grace laughed. "Maybe that's why I'm so clumsy—there aren't toys scattered on the deck, but I keep trying to dodge them anyway."

Spence laughed with her, then asked more quietly, "Train pieces and toys? You've got kids? Or…"

Grace prepared herself for his quick exit, as had happened at every singles activity in recent memory. "Just one. Aaron. He's just turned seven." She fought the urge to hold her breath. These awkward moments were exactly why she stayed away from singles events.

"If he looks anything like his mom, I'm sure he's adorable." Spence caught himself checking her out, especially the way she bit her lower lip. Her straight white teeth sparkled. He reminded himself—as a dentist—it was his job to notice these things.

Grace blushed. "Well, thank you. He does look like me, but more like his dad. That's a good thing, though—hopefully he won't be the shortest boy in his class." She returned to scrubbing the splatter on his shirt, trying not to stare at his bare chest... or think too hard about the fact he hadn't bolted upon learning she had a child.

"So... you've been married?" Spence asked, hesitating.

Grace sighed and scrubbed harder. He was disappointed. Of course he was. She'd never see him again once the shirt was clean. "Yeah. A little over six years ago. We pretty much got pregnant on the honeymoon. The marriage... it just didn't make it. We got divorced early last year—probably about four years later than we should have."

Spence nodded slowly. "I was married, too. She decided the Church wasn't for her. And... well, that meant I wasn't either."

Grace froze. Slowly, she looked up. Her eyes widened. Divorced?

"Uh, really? I'm so sorry..." she said, her voice quieter now. Another divorcee. Her brain struggled to process it.

He gave her a sheepish grin. "Yeah. It's not easy, huh? Especially at singles events. I feel like I've got a big 'REJECTED' tag hanging around my neck. And that I'm past my sell-by date to boot."

Grace chuckled, tension she hadn't noticed slowly melting from her shoulders. "I understand that. I feel like saying, 'Hi, I'm Grace and I was sent back defective. Wanna date me?'"

Spence's eyes sparkled. "That's about right! The girls flee when I say 'ex-wife' faster than I can blink."

"Try saying something about your kid. Guys will start gnawing their arms off just to get out of dancing with me. I might as well have a giant scarlet letter on my chest." She hesitated. "Did you two... do you have any children?"

"Nope. Just lots of nieces and nephews. My ex didn't want kids." He stopped short of saying "or maybe just not with me," but the sadness in his expression said it for him.

Right then, the door opened. Megs and McKay returned, chattering and laughing, barely noticing Grace and Spence. McKay handed over Spence's clean clothes, took Megs' hand, and disappeared just as fast. Neither said a word.

As soon as the door clicked shut, Grace and Spence burst out laughing.

"I don't know either of them very well, but they seem to have met their match," Grace giggled.

"I almost feel sorry for her," Spence quipped. "He came on this cruise determined to find his eternal mate. I'm not sure how he'll pick just one girl, though. He always seems to have a flock, and he doesn't mind it one bit."

"From what she told me, she's hoping to find a husband. That girl has a way of cramming a *lot* of words into very short windows of time." Grace giggled again.

"Then maybe she'll give him a run for his money. I've always said they'd have to reinstate polygamy for him—not to break his heart, but to save the entire bevy of women who fall for him."

That sent Grace into a laughing fit so intense she grabbed her sides. "Don't even joke! I've always known there was a reason I was born when I was—and that's it. Well, that and I really like air conditioning."

"Oh, you *know* you want to be wife number four and get the Tuesday time slot. Admit it, Grace."

"That's it! You asked for it, mister." Grace lunged at him, grabbing a pillow. "I'm a mom, and moms are superior pillow fighters!"

Spence begged for mercy between fits of laughter. Both were a little surprised at themselves—but neither stopped.

"Say... Peter Piper picked a peck of polygamy princesses!" Grace teased.

Spence laughed and lost his balance. "Peter Piper—oh, forget it!" He grabbed her wrists, pulled her arms behind her back, and tossed the pillow aside. Holding her wrists in one hand, he scrubbed his knuckles into her scalp.

"Now say, 'Please, Spence, I'd *love* to be your polygamy princess!'"

"OW! Not on your life! Okay! Okay! UNCLE!" Grace shrieked through laughter. "Let me go—I can't breathe!"

He released her and collapsed on the floor beside her, gasping for air and wiping tears from his cheeks.

After a pause, Spence turned to her. "So... will you have dinner with me tonight? Just relax, avoid my cousin and your roommate, and hide from all the other singles looking for eternal companions."

Grace blinked. The change in tone caught her off guard.

Spence smiled. "Besides, any woman who can survive a knuckle noogie and not worry about her hair? Definitely worth getting to know better."

Grace found herself smiling back. "Then yes. I'd love to. Honestly, that's the most fun I've had with another adult in ages. Who knew when McKay helped me with my luggage I'd end up wrestling with his cousin?"

She paused. "I wonder what those two are up to."

"Who knows. Wait—he helped you with your luggage? He actually *did* that?" Spence chuckled. "I thought he was kidding."

"Huh?" Grace looked confused.

"The luggage thing. That was Mick's pick-up line for the ladies as they boarded."

"Well... it worked. Sort of. He was my hero." Grace grimaced, remembering the struggle with her suitcase. "Think he'll do the same when we leave?" She half-grinned.

"Depends on if he's found his eternal companion. But I'd be glad to help you," Spence offered.

"Sold. You certainly look strong enough." Grace gave him a quick once-over, hoping he didn't notice her lingering admiration.

"Alright. I'll let you get ready." Spence pulled on his clean, dry t-shirt and grabbed the soiled one. "I'll stop by at seven?"

"I'll be ready," Grace said—and to her own surprise, she meant it.

Chapter 10

McKay threw open the cabin door and shouted, "I'm in love! I'm in LOVE!"

Spence rolled his eyes as he opened a drawer, looking for socks. "Who is it this hour? Blonde? Brunette? Redhead?" You never could tell with McKay.

"Please, Spence. Give me a break. I'm not like that." McKay dropped onto his bed, shoving his duffel bag onto the floor. He folded his hands behind his head and leaned back with a sigh.

"Uh... Cuz... I hate to break it to you, but yeah, you are. I can't count on one hand how many women you dated the weekend before we came on this cruise." Spence sat on the edge of his bed to put on his socks. He was freshly dressed in a pair of khaki shorts and a bright blue polo shirt.

McKay moved one hand from behind his head and clutched his chest. "I'm wounded. Really. I can't believe you'd say such a thing!"

"I can't believe you're being so dramatic. Maybe if you spent more than an hour with a girl before moving to the next one..."

"Spence, really. I just want to make sure I choose well. I mean, there are so many women, and it's going to take a special woman to be my bride and raise our twelve kids."

A snort erupted from Spence. "A special woman indeed. To put up with you!"

McKay got up and grabbed his cousin from behind. "Take that back! You know I'm a delight to live with!"

The two wrestled, bumping into beds and chairs as Spence laughed, "Oh right. Perhaps I should tell the future Mrs. Grant about how you—"

"Oh, you won't be telling anyone anything!" McKay grunted, trying to stop Spence's escape.

"Yeah, I will," Spence gasped. Neither of them would give in, but both were clearly getting worn out wrestling in the limited space of their cabin.

"Give it up, old man. You're old, you're gray—hey, are you going bald?"

"WHAT?!" Spence stopped short in mock horror, and in the moment of distraction, McKay tackled him.

"I knew that would get you! Ha! Go ahead, make fun of me—guess I showed you!" McKay chuckled good-naturedly.

"Let me up. You're messing up my clothes. And my hair. I just got dressed and..." Spence squirmed under McKay.

"Hey yeah, I noticed you were looking all spiffy. Got a hot date?" McKay scoffed.

"As a matter of fact..." Spence began. It wasn't really a date, but if it got McKay off his back...

McKay leapt off his cousin. "No way, Cuz! You got yourself a date? Nu-uh! Is the world coming to an end?"

Spence stood up slowly, smoothing his shirt and picking stray lint off. "Please. I go with you to all those ward activities. I see women all the time."

"Yeah, but you don't DATE them. You know what, I need to sit down. I can't believe it." McKay stumbled back dramatically and dropped onto his bed.

Spence said nothing, but a smile tugged at the corners of his mouth. He tried not to think too hard about Grace. About how easy it had been to talk with her. How he hadn't felt awkward. How she'd actually laughed. He reminded himself it wasn't a date. Just dinner. Just company. Still, his chest felt lighter than it had in a while.

"So, who are you in love with now?" Spence asked, smoothly changing the subject. "It's been like two minutes, Cuz."

"Oh, just—I'm in love with the week. It's gonna be great. I was walking on one of the upper decks and saw so many pretty women... all sailing with us!" McKay's grin couldn't have been goofier if he tried.

Spence fought the urge to roll his eyes. He should've known. His cousin was in love with the idea that there were a hundred beautiful women to flirt with. And for McKay, that was practically heaven.

Chapter 11

Grace could not believe what Paige had considered "must-have"—and what she'd somehow left out. She looked at the disaster zone that was her bed and debated calling FEMA. There wasn't a single thing in that beast of a suitcase Grace felt comfortable cramming herself into for dinner. And she still couldn't believe she'd agreed to dinner with that man.

Her face flushed. Not only had she dumped a cold drink on him—a complete stranger—he had also been, well... handsome. And she'd then proceeded to act like a complete dork.

Her thoughts circled relentlessly. Handsome. There she went again. She needed to stop thinking about Spence like that. She wasn't here for this. Not to talk to strangers or flirt or pretend she was someone she wasn't. She'd had her shot at marriage, and it didn't exactly go well. Now, she was a mom. There were more important things to think about than attractive men with easy smiles.

What must he think of her? Could she have acted any more ridiculous? She was hopeless around men. There was a reason she never had good dates—she couldn't function like a sane human being around them.

She had showered, washed her hair, and torn through a suitcase that contained enough clothes for a three-week vacation. Nothing looked right. Maybe Spence would change his mind after replaying the bizarre episode with the drink and the frantic stain removal. Grace glanced at the clock. She was running out of time.

With a groan, she closed her eyes, reached into the chaos, and grabbed the first thing her fingers touched. She opened her eyes: a brightly colored sundress. The blue in the fabric brought out the color of her eyes. Well... that was promising. Without another thought, she dropped her bathrobe and pulled it on.

Surveying the mess again, she debated cleaning it up. Instead, she grabbed an armload of clothes and stuffed them into the suitcase. Problem solved—for now. Tonight, she might have to sleep curled around the overstuffed case, but she'd deal with that later.

She gave her hair one last brush. It was, as usual, not quite curly, not quite straight. Just sort of... there. Unmanageable. She shoved on a headband to keep it out of her face and hoped for the best. Her last good hair day had definitely been sometime before Aaron was born. He got all the good hair. Hormones, she figured.

A bit of powder to blot the shiny spots, a dash of clear gloss—done. Grace had no illusions about herself. She wasn't going to win any beauty contests, but she didn't want to scare anyone either. She had a girl-next-door look that made men feel like she was more sister than siren. A little notice to drop twenty pounds would've been nice, but it was too late now.

Still, Spence had asked her to dinner. Spence. Handsome. Funny. And—miracle of miracles—a church member. She didn't expect anything serious, not even a friendship really, but it might be nice to have someone to talk to on this trip. Someone who didn't make her feel like a walking cautionary tale.

A knock on the door interrupted her spiraling thoughts. She gave herself one last once-over—checking for stray hairs, random food smudges, or surprise blemishes—and opened the door.

Spence stood in the hallway, freshly dressed and waiting. She glanced at her watch. Seven o'clock. Right on time.

"Wow," he said, looking into her eyes. "You look amazing."

"Thank you." Grace blushed, making a mental note to thank Paige for helping her pack. "You look very handsome yourself. And I promise to try not to ruin your shirt this time... but only if you promise not to make me dance in these shoes."

Spence glanced down at her feet. Citrine open-toed sandals with chunky heels. No wonder she looked taller than he remembered.

"I'm not usually a heels person," she confessed. "I'm hoping to manage walking. Dancing might be pushing it."

"We'll see." He winked and took her hand. "Come on."

"Spencer, I'm serious," she warned, just as she caught the edge of the transition strip between hallway and deck.

"Whoa!" He caught her before she could fall. "Okay, I promise. No dancing. Grace, do you want to go back and change your shoes?"

"No," she muttered, still blushing. "I don't have anything else that matches this dress. Sorry about that. It wasn't intentional." She gently pulled her hand back.

"All right." He gestured down the hallway. "Dinner awaits."

They walked together, each secretly wondering what the evening might hold.

Chapter 12

Grace held her plate in one hand and stared at the mounds of shrimp, plates of fish, and various other seafood selections spread across the long buffet. She loved seafood, but didn't get to eat it very often.

"Wow, I don't know where to start," Spence said behind her.

Grace smiled. "I know, I was just thinking the same thing. It's like... sensory overload. My eyes, my nose... my stomach..." A grumble from her abdomen confirmed the last one.

"Sounds like you've brought your appetite. That's good— looks like we'll need it!" Spence gave Grace a toothy grin and nudged her forward. "Just grab something and keep going. Once you start, it gets easier."

Grace watched as Spence scooped some boiled shrimp onto his plate. "Did it help?"

"Sure did! Next up—whatever that is." He pointed at a tray of seasoned fish and added it to his plate.

Taking the cue, Grace grabbed the nearest tongs and placed a few boiled shrimp on her plate as well. It helped. With each item she added, her nerves settled slightly.

They worked their way down the buffet line, piling their plates so full they had to walk carefully to avoid spilling. Grace's plate held lobster, shrimp, fish, fried calamari, and scallops. She glanced at Spence's plate—easily double the size of hers. If she'd missed anything, he hadn't.

They sat and unfolded their napkins. Grace tried to suppress the butterflies in her stomach. Dinner with a man was never simple. With dinner came conversation, and that was where things usually fell apart. She stumbled, over-explained, said something weird...

"Grace, would you like to bless the food?" Spence asked quietly.

Her head snapped up. She'd never been on a date where someone brought up prayer. In her usual routine, a silent "Bless this food" would suffice. But in a dining room full of Latter-day Saints, bowed heads weren't exactly unusual.

"Um... sure..." She folded her arms and bowed her head, murmuring a simple blessing for the food and their trip. On impulse, she added thanks for new friends. When she opened her eyes, Spence was smiling at her.

"Thank you, Grace," he said, forcing his gaze back to his plate. The prayer was simple, but sincere. And the mention of friends felt... safe. He liked safe.

They ate in silence for a moment. Spence tried to think of something to say—small talk had never been his strength. Dating had always been hard, before and after his marriage.

Grace noticed a flicker of sadness cross his face. "Are you okay?"

"What? Oh—yeah." Spence startled, surprised she'd noticed. He tried to focus on his food.

Grace tried to recover. "It's just... I hope the food's okay?"

"Oh, the food's fine." He paused, hesitant. "It's just..."

The words wouldn't come. It had only been six months since the divorce was finalized, but sometimes it felt like yesterday. The pain wasn't as sharp, but it still showed up when he least expected it.

"You don't have to explain," Grace said gently. "You don't even know me. It's okay."

"No, it's... it's just a long story. You probably didn't come on this trip to hear about someone's baggage."

"Actually, it wasn't my idea to come on this trip," Grace replied with a small laugh. "My friends kind of made me."

"Your friends made you?" Spence tilted his head, grateful for the change of topic.

"They ambushed me at a girl's night out. Bought the ticket. Packed my bags. Dropped me at the airport with no way to get home."

Spence chuckled. "Well, that's some mighty nice friends—leaving you defenseless and alone to be gobbled up by McKay."

Grace laughed. "Right? They threw me to the wolves. They're all married now, so they think this kind of thing is fun."

Spence's smile faltered. "Yeah. I know how that feels."

A brief silence settled between them, not awkward—just heavy. Around them, the dining room buzzed with laughter and conversation. It seemed easy for everyone else. Grace set her fork down.

"Spence," she said softly, "I know we're both divorced. I don't know your story, and I won't pry. But I get it. I hate this—starting over. Doing this 'single' thing again."

He looked up, surprised by her candor.

"My marriage... was a mess," Grace continued. "Too young. Too fast. We jumped into everything—marriage, a baby, a house—and eventually, it just... crumbled. He had a girlfriend. I think it was over long before that, but we hung on for our son. Because that's what you're supposed to do."

Spence was quiet a moment. Then: "I came home early one night. Wanted to surprise my wife with dinner. Instead, I found her packing her car. She said she was done—with me, with the Church, with everything. She wanted to live her life."

He paused. "She called me last week. She's getting remarried. Having a baby. She's moved on. Sometimes it feels like the world did, too—and forgot to take me with it."

"I know that feeling," Grace whispered. "My friends are on baby number three. My ex goes on more dates in a month than I've been on in three years."

Spence managed a smile. "I always thought I'd have kids. Still want them. Just... not in the cards, I guess."

"Tell me about your son?" he asked.

Grace lit up. "He's seven. Wild. Right before I left, he built me this huge Lego boat. He's obsessed with Legos, dinosaurs, Buzz Lightyear..."

Spence laughed. "When I was his age, I was obsessed with firemen. I had the whole setup—jacket, hat, toy truck. Drove my mom nuts."

Grace grinned. "Oh yeah? My son tried to fly off the table last month yelling 'To infinity and beyond!' I was sure we were headed to the ER."

They laughed together, more relaxed now.

"All right," Grace said, mock-serious. "Let's get the rest of the awkward stuff out of the way. I'm Grace. Divorced. Mom. Photo lab worker. Not allowed near X-Acto knives. I was the Primary chorister until recently. My bishop wants me to be the Singles rep—hilarious, right? Oh, and I live near Chapel Hill. Anything else?"

Spence raised a brow. "Well, it's a Singles cruise. I think I'm supposed to ask your shoe size, dress size, and ring size. McKay's already proposed to three women."

Grace gaped at him, then laughed as she tried to smack his hand—accidentally knocking his drink. He caught it with the other hand.

"I'm learning to stay alert around you," he teased.

"You mean to avoid becoming the next victim of a Grace-catastrophe?"

"Is that what we're calling it now?"

"Well, it sounds better than klutz."

Spence chuckled. "All right. My turn, then?"

"Yep. Age, rank, and serial number, mister."

Grace tried to look stern, but she couldn't help grinning.

Chapter 13

"So, how many brothers and sisters do you have?" Spence and Grace settled into a slow dance, courtesy of McKay's insistence they not miss the typical "get to know everyone" event.

"One of each," Grace looked up at Spence. She decided she was jealous of his long, thick eyelashes. Even mascara couldn't give her those. "How about you?"

"You only have ONE of each? Wow, I'm one of nine. I have eight sisters. I fall at number six. Being the only boy, I did manage to snag my own room after a few years, though, so it worked out for me!" Spence laughed, remembering the arguments among his sisters—sometimes drawing visible lines to divide their rooms. "Only three of you? I just couldn't imagine."

"Me either. Nine. Wow. Spence, how'd you get through it? I mean, the PMS had to be constant—and you being the only boy..."

Spence let out a hearty laugh. "That room I told you about? I stayed there a lot. It was safer. Sometimes my dad would hide with me and we'd watch baseball. Said us men had to stick together!"

Grace tightened her hold on his shoulder for a second, biting back laughter. "I can see that. You were so outnumbered!"

"No joke we were outnumbered. I never got to use the phone either. If one sister wasn't on talking about boys, makeup, or shoes? Another one was!"

"Guess you didn't get to ask a lot of girls out then as a teenager!" Grace tried to fight the giggles, but picturing Spence as a hapless teen boy surrounded by sisters was too much.

"And the shoes... and purses... everywhere! All I wanted was a basketball!"

"Yeah I remember being a teenager. That's all you young men were good for! Every week in the gym, there you guys were playing basketball. We had to do service projects and activities to earn our medallions. And you guys? Basketball!"

"Hey! We have a lot of energy and need SOME way to use it up!" Spence grinned. "What did you WANT us to do?"

"Um, I don't know? Scout-y stuff?"

"Well, I did get my Eagle. So, I was a GOOD boy scout. Always prepared. My father was an Eagle Scout too, actually. When I was in young men's, he was assistant scoutmaster. Guess I didn't have much of a chance to slack, did I?"

They danced in silence for a moment.

"I did enjoy my family though. I loved having so many siblings, even if they were all girls. I did have plenty of cousins who were boys to make up for all the sisters."

"A lot of cousins too? Just how big IS your family?"

"Both my parents were one of ten. So there were more than enough cousins. I've never tried counting them all, though..."

Grace inwardly shuddered. "Are you kidding? Did all your aunts and uncles have large families, too?"

"Yeah, most of them. I guess that's why I've always wanted a big family."

Grace hesitated. "Uh, how many kids do you want someday?"

"Oh, at least ten," Spence said with a straight face. Seeing her stunned expression, he added, "But since I'd have to marry an eighteen-year-old this week and immediately start churning out babies for that to happen... I know I should lower my expectations. Can you imagine me marrying your roommate?"

Grace laughed nervously. "No, I can't. I can't see myself marrying a kid like your cousin either."

"You can't do that. I called dibs," Spence blushed, realizing he spoke aloud.

"Oh really?"

"Well... he tried. Told me he saw you first. Then I flexed my caveman muscles and he backed off."

McKay appeared, leaning in with a date on his arm. "That's Nephite muscles, not caveman. Spence wanted to be Nephi when he grows up, did he tell you?"

Spence glared while Grace grinned. "Honestly, Spence, I think you're blushing!"

Spence pretended to pout. "Even if you don't want to marry me and have ten kids."

Grace's heart skipped at the M word. "Not on your life. I hope your mom had an epidural for fifteen years straight."

The song ended. Spence offered, "Want to get some punch?"

"Please don't tell me that's what you really do on dates!"

"Of course! Red punch, white cookies, Church videos, and Pictionary!"

"Well, I didn't date many church members. My ex-husband wasn't a member."

"That must have been hard."

"Yeah... it was..." Grace grew quiet.

Spence handed her a cup of punch and grabbed one for himself.

"I'm kind of tired," Grace said. "I think I should turn in."

"I'll walk you back," Spence offered, tossing their cups and gently touching her back.

Spence decided to say goodnight and leave it at that. His heart wasn't ready.

Across the dance floor, McKay watched them go, ideas forming. Spence needed a push. He grinned to himself and turned back to the crowd of women waiting for their turn to dance.

Chapter 14

Grace returned to her cabin after an unexpectedly powerful Sunday service. She missed her son, but the quiet reverence without noisy children running around had been... refreshing. It had been a long time since she felt the Spirit so clearly.

Some Sundays, Grace dreaded church—not because she didn't want to worship, but because it was hard to concentrate when wrangling a young child alone. But today? Today, she had truly feasted on the Gospel. And she hadn't realized how much she needed that until it filled her.

Her heart lighter than it had been in months, Grace offered a silent prayer of thanks—for the peace, the Spirit, and for her friends who pushed her to come on this cruise. She even found herself looking forward to their port day in Mexico tomorrow. Her first time out of the country.

She eyed her suitcase. Unpacking would be responsible. But the ocean breeze filtering through the balcony door whispered other ideas. The sea always called her, especially after years of living in North Carolina, near Emerald Isle. That salty air beat sorting through suitcases every single time.

Honoring the Sabbath had always been a goal, though not always an easy one. Her boss did his best with scheduling, but Sundays weren't guaranteed. Even when she was off, there was laundry, errands, and all the little things that came with parenting solo. But not today. Today, she had time. And quiet. And stillness. She grabbed her scriptures, a magazine she'd picked up in the airport, and headed toward the bathroom to change.

She tied her sarong over a modest one-piece suit—probably wouldn't swim, but better to be prepared—and washed off the light makeup from that morning. Pulling her hair into a ponytail, she looked up just as the door opened.

"Hey! Wasn't that just the best service?" Megs breezed in, kicking off her pumps. "I really enjoyed it!"

Grace gave her a polite smile and reached for her book and magazine. "It was really wonderful. It's been a long time since I've been able to actually concentrate in Sacrament."

Megs flopped onto her bed and started rummaging through her bag. "I bet. It must be hard, being a single mom. Is his father... in your ward?"

Grace hesitated. "Actually... he's not a member. So no, I don't see him at church."

"Oh. How long have you been divorced?"

"Over a year. We split up more than two years ago. It wasn't a good marriage." Grace tried to keep her tone neutral, hoping to avoid a deeper conversation. The past was... the past.

Megs nodded, digging for a change of clothes. "I guess you must be ready to move on, though, if you're here. I saw you went to dinner with that Spence guy."

Grace blinked. "Well, I wouldn't say I'm trying to move on. I'm getting past the divorce, sure—but I'm not looking for a relationship. This whole trip? Was my friends' idea."

"But you two looked so good together!" Megs grinned. "I don't know his story, but wow... he's HOT. You should totally go find him and hang out with him again!"

Grace stared at her, stunned. She wasn't sure what to make of Megs' tone or suggestion.

"Seriously," Megs continued. "If he's as nice as he is hot, what do you have to lose? You better snag him before someone else does!"

"Uh... no." Grace shook her head firmly. "We just had dinner. We didn't know anyone else. It was... nice. But I'm not chasing anyone. I have a child to think about—and honestly?

I'm tired. I don't have the time or energy to deal with men and all their... baggage."

She folded her arms and fixed Megs with a steady look. "I'm actually happy being single. It's hard sometimes, yeah. But Aaron's happy. And I'm doing okay. I don't have time to date, and what little time I do have? I use it to rest."

Megs looked chastened. "I'm sorry. I didn't mean to offend you."

"It's okay. Really. I know you meant well." Grace softened, grabbing her things. "I'm just going to go read and enjoy the ocean for a bit. I'll see you later."

"Hey, maybe just be his friend?" Megs called after her.

Grace paused. "Maybe. If I run into him again, we'll see. But I'm not going out of my way." She opened the door and peeked into the hall—no Spence in sight. Good. She slipped out quickly, grateful for the excuse to walk toward the deck and let the sea wind clear her thoughts.

Chapter 15

McKay and Spence returned to their room after morning services in silence, each lost in private thoughts. Spence loosened his tie as they stepped inside. McKay kicked off his shoes with a sigh of contentment.

He tossed his tie onto his luggage and flopped onto the bed. "Cuz, some of the stuff they said... wow. I'm actually really looking forward to the tour tomorrow."

Spence chuckled. "I knew it! You can't mock me now. You finally realize how cool all this is."

"Okay, okay, no need to act so triumphant." McKay shot him a look. "It's gonna be totally awesome."

"Hey, I'm just saying... I know you. You only came hoping to flirt with girls, and now you're starting to appreciate the rest of it."

"Mr. Smarty Pants over here," McKay grumbled. "Think you know everything, huh? You're not so perfect either. Is that a little pride I detect?"

Spence smiled, but his expression turned serious. "I never said I was perfect. I'm far from it."

McKay sat up, surprised. "Hey man, I'm sorry."

"It's okay," Spence said quietly. "I guess I just never realized how much I must've messed things up. Not until Julie..."

He trailed off, the weight of unresolved questions settling between them.

"Oh, Spence, you dummy. That wasn't you. You doted on Julie. None of us really know what happened there—but it wasn't your fault. And hey, girls dig you. Look at that Grace chick."

Spence met his cousin's gaze, then shook his head. "That was nothing. We just had dinner. It was nice to know I'm not the only divorced person here. I bet she felt the same."

"Whatever. She's into you. You must be blind if you didn't notice."

Spence considered that. "She's beautiful. And she's been through a lot. I'm sure she'd like someone with a little less baggage than me."

"Spence, wake up. She's not the only girl who's ever liked you. And I'm sure she—"

"Yeah, and look what the last girl did. She liked me, all right—right up until the day she left. I just can't do that again." He slowly pulled off one of his dress shoes, methodical and pensive.

McKay ran a hand through his hair. "What, are you kidding me? So just because Julie lost her mind, you're gonna pass on someone who's into you—and who you clearly like? That's not logical."

"Don't talk about her like that," Spence said. "I don't know why she did what she did, but I'm sure she had her reasons."

"I just hate how she hurt you, that's all. Don't miss out on something good just because of the past. It's not fair—to you, or to anyone else." McKay's voice softened. "You deserve better than staying stuck."

Spence exhaled slowly. "I'm not planning to see Grace again. It's better this way. I'm not interested in starting anything. I told you that before we even got on this cruise."

"Then fine," McKay said. "Just be friendly. It wouldn't kill you to talk to someone besides me at all these group activities."

Spence gave a half-smile. "You might be right. But I'm not going out of my way. If I happen to see her, that's one thing. I'd rather just relax, study my scriptures, and walk the sites. I'm trying to keep things simple."

McKay leaned against the wall, watching him. "That's fair. But you should ask her to come on tomorrow's excursion with us."

Spence raised an eyebrow. "Are you planning to invite someone?"

"Obviously." McKay grinned. "You don't want to be a third wheel, do you?"

Spence rolled his eyes. His cousin's threat wasn't empty—that was exactly the type of thing McKay would do. "I'm not going out of my way," he repeated. "It's Sunday. I need some quiet time to study and get ready for tomorrow."

He opened his Book of Mormon and settled onto the bed with purpose.

"Fine, I'll leave you to it. But if you see her—think about it. I'm going to see what's happening on the ship, meet some ladies, get something to eat... you know, the usual."

McKay grabbed some clean clothes, changed in record time, and was out the door with a wave.

Spence let the door close behind him and exhaled. He meant what he said. Life was too complicated right now. Even with a beautiful, kind, intelligent woman... it just wasn't the right time.

He shook his head and turned his focus back to the scriptures. A moment later, he retrieved his Institute manual from his suitcase and flipped it open beside the Book of Mormon. Soon, he was immersed in the world of Nephi—his cousin and the cruise around him forgotten.

Chapter 16

The alarm blared, yanking Spence out of a sound sleep. He sat up with a start and shut it off, blinking into the dim cabin light. In just a few hours, he would be walking the soil of Nephi's Promised Land.

"Augh," McKay groaned from beneath a nest of covers and pillows.

"Wake up, Cuz! It's time to get moving!" Spence leapt out of bed, already grabbing the clothes he had carefully laid out the night before.

"You have to be kidding me. What time is it?" McKay asked, voice thick with sleep.

"Time to get up!" Spence was half-dressed and buzzing with anticipation. He was as eager as a child on Christmas morning.

"I swear I just fell asleep," McKay grumbled, rubbing bleary eyes. "You set the alarm too early."

"No, you just stayed out too late. What were you doing? It was Sunday!"

"I was hanging out—with people. Having fun. Remember fun?" McKay stumbled into the bathroom.

"I was getting ready for today—reading the Book of Mormon, reviewing the itinerary, reading the site pamphlets. I wanted to be prepared." Spence tucked his pale polo shirt into his khaki shorts. "And yes, I do remember fun—I just don't always agree with your definition."

"You've read the Book of Mormon more times than the prophet at this point," McKay called from the bathroom.

"How much more prepared can you be? You should've hung out with me."

"You can never be too prepared, Cuz. And I know exactly what you were doing. Flirting. How many girls was it last night—two? Five? Ten?"

McKay stepped out and gave him a look. "I don't know what you're talking about. For your information, I was having a spiritual conversation."

"Right." Spence raised an eyebrow. "Did it include how some girl must've been hurt when she fell from heaven?"

"Ugh, that's tacky. I'd never say something like that," McKay huffed, rooting through his duffel bag.

"Oh, right. It must've been about how you're just sure you knew her in the preexistence."

"You better—"

"Don't even pretend you haven't used that one," Spence cut in with a grin.

McKay pointed a mock-warning finger. "At least I talk to women. I don't hide from them."

"I don't hide from women."

"Uh-huh." McKay held up one finger. "Let's count how many women you've talked to since we got on this ship. Hmm. There's Grace... and—wait for it—yep, still just Grace."

Spence swallowed. Hearing her name sent a strange flush through his body. He hadn't seen her yesterday—not that he'd tried. That was fine. Totally fine. But it didn't explain why his pulse had just sped up.

"I was studying. I told you that," he said quietly.

"Uh-huh," McKay replied, drawing the words out with amused suspicion as he yanked on his clothes.

"That's all it was," Spence insisted. "Didn't we already have this conversation yesterday? Come on, let's go."

"Sure, sure," McKay said, rubbing his stomach. "Let's get some grub. I'm starving."

He shoved his feet into untied sneakers and followed Spence toward the door. Their usual banter filled the small room, but McKay noticed something different today. Spence had a spark again—a quiet hum of excitement he hadn't seen in a long time.

Maybe there was hope for his heartbroken cousin after all.

Chapter 17

Grace raced around her cabin, still half-asleep. She'd missed the alarm and wasn't sure there'd be time for breakfast if she wanted to make it to the day's tour.

She shoved her feet into the first pair of sandals she could find, grabbed a ponytail holder, and jammed it into her small travel purse. Snatching her camera bag on the way out, she bolted from the room, heart pounding as she checked the time again.

As she jogged down the hallway, she muttered a quick prayer that she wouldn't miss the excursion. Visiting Mexico had been the one part of the cruise she'd truly looked forward to. She had never been out of the country before, and the tour promised fascinating cultural and historical stops she couldn't wait to photograph.

Grace arrived breathless at the meeting point, where a throng of people were organizing into smaller groups. She blinked at the chaos, trying to make sense of the clustering until a young woman with a clipboard approached her.

"You just made it," the woman said. "What's your name?"

"Grace Jackson," Grace panted, brushing a hand through her unruly hair.

"Jackson, Jackson... Ah! Here we go." The woman scanned her list and then pointed toward a loosely gathered group nearby. "You're with Group C, just over there."

"Thanks!" Grace said, already hurrying off before the woman could say anything more.

As she approached the group, one of the men turned—and Grace felt her face flush with recognition.

McKay.

He lit up the moment he saw her and leaned toward the person beside him.

"Mic, what—?" Spence began, distracted, then froze mid-sentence as he looked up and saw her.

Grace stopped short. "Um... hi." Her voice sounded small. She hadn't expected to run into either of them—and certainly not first thing in the morning. Her pulse quickened, and she tried to calm herself with a deep breath.

"Come on over and hang out with us," McKay said cheerfully, slinging an arm around her and drawing her into their space between him and Spence. "Stick by us—we'll have some fun!"

Spence looked over Grace's head at McKay, alarm in his eyes. "Yeah... fun," he managed, his voice cracking slightly.

Grace blushed again. She hadn't meant to intrude and, judging from Spence's reaction, maybe she had. She started to backpedal. "Oh, it's okay. You don't—"

"But of course we do!" McKay cut her off. "Besides, Spence probably knows more about this place than the tour guide. You know you wanna stick with us." He winked at her.

Grace glanced at Spence. He hesitated, then gave a slow nod. "Yeah. Stay with us."

He sounded hesitant, but Grace smiled, grateful for the invitation—awkward or not.

Spence, meanwhile, had a sinking suspicion his cousin was playing matchmaker again. He made a mental list of possible ways to get even.

"Okay," Grace said, settling into her spot. "But I really didn't want to—"

"Great!" McKay interrupted again, clapping his hands. "Here we go! Off on the adventure of a lifetime!"

Spence shot him a look that clearly said, What are you thinking? But McKay ignored him, practically bouncing with smug satisfaction.

For McKay, this was perfect. Grace's presence would nudge Spence out of his shell, help him relax. And maybe, just maybe, help him heal.

Spence wasn't so sure. Yes, a part of him—the part he didn't like to admit existed—was thrilled to see Grace again. But the rest of him? The part still scarred and wary?

That part wanted no complications.

And Grace... was definitely a complication.

Chapter 18

"Nephi!" Spence squeezed his eyes shut and exhaled slowly. "I just can't believe I'm moments away from walking on what could actually be the same ground Nephi trod when he first arrived in the promised land. I feel like... like a teenager on his first date or something—just... giddy."

McKay laughed, while Grace tried her best to ignore the word date. It was endearing to see someone so overcome with joy about the Gospel, but romance was the last thing she wanted to think about. She and McKay stepped off the dock with the rest of the tour group, the sun already warming the pavement beneath their feet.

Spence, too swept up in the moment to notice his own phrasing, took in a deep breath of salty air and slowly let it out. "This is so awesome."

He opened his eyes, stepped off the dock and onto land, a wide grin overtaking his face. His heart leapt. His lifelong dream—to experience the places described in the Book of Mormon—was finally real.

"Was it everything you thought it would be?" McKay asked, rolling his eyes but tossing Grace a quick wink.

Grace ignored the wink and kept her attention on Spence.

Spence inhaled again, eyes dancing as he turned to them. "It's just so incredible. This air, this land—this is it, you guys. The Book of Mormon. It all happened here."

Grace felt a warmth blossom inside her. Surprisingly, it wasn't awkward to share in Spence's sacred moment. Instead, she felt honored. Quietly, she raised her camera and snapped a photo of him, catching his radiant expression. She made a mental note to give him a copy once she developed the film. Moments like these were rare—worth remembering.

She adjusted her focus and clicked another picture, just to be safe.

McKay shook his head. "What, right here on this very spot? The whole thing happened right here?" he teased. "You're gonna miss the really spiritual stuff—like beachfront shopping and overpriced hotel coffee."

Spence broke into a grin and looked around at the towering hotels and sunbathing tourists. "Okay, fine, maybe this isn't exactly what Nephi saw. But use your imagination! Come on, McKay—you just don't get it. It's so..."

"It's okay," Grace said gently. "I understand. There are moments in life that hit different. You're allowed to soak it in. But let's go before our group leaves us behind."

Spence turned to her, visibly grateful, and matched her smile. "Thanks. It's just... I've wanted this for so long. To come here. To experience this. I've always loved the Book of Mormon, and it's wild to think how close all of this is to where I grew up in Virginia. The Bible stories always felt so far away. But this? It's vivid. Tangible. And now..."

"Now you're here," Grace finished softly. "Honestly? Being here with you—I'm getting more excited for the tour. I already wanted to see everything, but your enthusiasm? It's kind of contagious."

Spence's expression softened, touched by her words.

"Oh geez, you two!" McKay groaned from ahead of them. "Enough with the Book of Mormon bonding. You haven't even seen anything yet!"

Spence laughed, snapping back to the present. "He's right. I should probably settle down before I get too emotional to take pictures."

"There's a whole day of adventure ahead," Grace said.

And together, the three of them hurried to catch up with the tour.

Chapter 19

Grace studied her camera display, astonished at how much film she'd already used. "I seriously need to get a digital camera."

"You're on what? Your 100th roll of film?" McKay teased.

She laughed, "It sure feels like it. I'm not sure I brought enough film. It's only the first excursion, and I've already used two and a half rolls—before lunch!"

"It's just so awe-inspiring. I can't believe we're here." Spence took a photograph as well. Since reaching the ruins, Grace's constant snapping of pictures reminded Spence to use his camera. He wanted pictures to remember the trip, but the various ruins kept distracting him. His own excitement drove most thoughts from his mind, and he moved about like an ADHD squirrel on caffeine.

They stood in front of the majestic Temple of Kukulcán at Chichén Itzá. The pyramid's grandeur was captivating, its steep steps reaching toward the sky.

"It's amazing, the architecture," Grace breathed.

"Hey, they ripped it off the Egyptians! Those copycats!" McKay joked.

Spence smacked him lightly on the back of the head. "Ow!"

"That's what you get, dork!" Spence exclaimed in mock frustration.

"I'm a dork? You're the one..." McKay started, only to have Grace cut him off.

"So, Nephi, when are you going to climb up to see the Temple?" Grace gave Spence an impish grin.

"Good question. It does sound right up your alley, Cuz! Even as steep as it is." McKay shielded his eyes with a hand and peered to the top of the seventy-nine-foot pyramid.

"McKay, you're rubbing off on Grace. Shazam, guys, there's nothing wrong with enjoying the Book of Mormon and trying to delve into the Scriptures. Even the prophet agrees with me. As for climbing to the top, maybe I'll just go now since apparently all you want to do is pick on me!" Spence tried his best to look wounded and pout, but McKay and Grace were not ready to buy his act.

"Oh, you know you love me, Spence. I'm your favorite cousin, right? I would never pick on you!" McKay gave a wide, innocent smile.

"Oh no, not you." Spence's voice dripped with sarcasm as he crossed his arms.

McKay blatantly ignored his cousin's attitude, asking Grace, "What about you? You going to climb to the top to see the Temple?"

"If I can make that climb, yeah! Ninety-one steps though? Yikes! I'm not sure I can do that!" Grace definitely was not in the greatest physical shape, and looking once more at the Pyramid of Kukulcán standing in front of her, she felt intimidated.

"I think you can do it. Besides, I bet Nephi here could use some company!" McKay nodded his head and jerked a thumb in Spence's direction.

"Har har, you two. If that's the way you're going to be..." Spence started toward the pyramid with a determined look on his face.

Grace called after him, "Hey, wait, Spence. I'm sorry, I was only joking around."

"It's OK," Spence mumbled and continued walking. He expected this kind of kidding from his cousin. McKay might be fine with constant kidding with women, but sometimes it could bring back the feelings of rejection Spence often dealt with.

"He'll be OK. You should follow him, go on," McKay whispered, encouraging Grace to tag along.

"What about you? What are you going to do? You're not going to go try to make the climb with your cousin?" Grace asked as she watched Spence worriedly.

"Oh, I'm sure I'll make it up there eventually. I'm going over there for now. I think I see your roommate, Megs." McKay pointed toward a cluster of young women, and Grace thought it did look like Megs.

"We'll catch up with you in a bit then?" Grace did not mean it to be a question.

"Totally. Enjoy the free time to look around and explore the ruins with Spence. Maybe you can get him to come back to the Twenty-First Century." McKay couldn't help but laugh. He hoped neither Grace nor Spence would notice his subtle attempt to give the two time alone together.

Chapter 20

Grace sprinted to catch up with Spence. She caught up with him, but at the expense of her own oxygen supply. Gasping for air was not really her idea of fun.

"You gonna come then?" Spence's voice was quiet.

"You don't mind, do you?" Grace suddenly felt a wave of self-conscious discomfort. Perhaps Spence did not want her horning in on his day and experiences.

"No, it's OK. I'm sorry. I... well, I don't expect you to understand. But in Seminary, I just fell in love with all the Book of Mormon stories, and I've always wanted to see these kinds of sights. It's just amazing to me. I shouldn't let my cousin get to me..." Spence trailed off. His excuses sounded lame, and he decided it was better to stop while he was ahead.

"I'm really sorry. I shouldn't have teased you. I mean, it is really cool to see all of this. I mean, it's breathtaking just seeing it, let alone thinking about the history. Spiritually, too. I... um... I don't want to intrude, but if you want the company..." She purposefully let her words trail off, not wanting to press Spence further.

He pondered her words for a moment and then stopped, turning to Grace. She almost tripped over her feet trying to avoid walking into him. His face softened as he looked into her eyes, and he tried to smile. "It's fine. Actually, some company would be nice."

Grace felt the relief wash over her. It made her feel good that he invited her, and she decided not to question it. "Ok...

so do you think there's an elevator?" She laughed, grateful when she saw Spence's smile.

"Well, you know, the Mayans were a very advanced culture focused on astronomy. Perhaps they also invented elevators. We could ask if you think you can't keep up..." He felt himself relax. Sometimes the light banter came a little easier.

"Oh, I'll keep up. Let's go!" Grace's eyes flashed in defiance of Spence's challenge.

As they approached the base of the pyramid, a tour guide's voice caught their attention. "Please remember, climbing the Temple of Kukulcán is prohibited. This measure protects the structure and ensures everyone's safety."

Spence turned to Grace, a hint of disappointment in his eyes.

"Looks like our climb ends here," she said, a hint of disappointment in her voice.

Spence nodded, his eyes fixed on the pyramid's summit. "Yeah, they stopped allowing climbs to protect the structure. Makes sense, but it's a bit disheartening."

They stood in silence, absorbing the grandeur of the temple. Each of the pyramid's four sides has 91 steps, and when you add the top platform, it totals 365—mirroring the days in a solar year .

"Did you know," Spence began, "during the spring and fall equinoxes, the setting sun casts shadows that create the illusion of a serpent slithering down the staircase? It's a tribute to Kukulcán, the feathered serpent deity."

Grace's eyes widened. "That's incredible. The Maya's understanding of astronomy was truly advanced."

Spence smiled. "Absolutely. They designed the pyramid so precisely that the light and shadow effect aligns perfectly during the equinoxes . It's a testament to their ingenuity."

They walked around the pyramid, taking in the intricate carvings and the serpent heads at the base of the northern staircase. Grace snapped photos, eager to capture the moment.

"Even without climbing, being here is surreal," she said. "It's like standing at the crossroads of history and spirituality."

Spence nodded. "Exactly. It's not just about reaching the top; it's about understanding and appreciating the significance of this place."

They found a shaded spot nearby and sat down, letting the atmosphere envelop them. The air was thick with history, and the whispers of the past seemed to dance around them.

Grace turned to Spence. "Thank you for sharing this with me. It's a memory I'll cherish forever."

He looked at her, his eyes reflecting the depth of his emotions. "Me too, Grace. Me too."

Chapter 21

Grace's stomach rumbled, reminding her the last thing she'd eaten was a piece of fruit back on the ship. The warm, humid air had suppressed her appetite for most of the morning, but now she knew she needed real food—and soon. Spence must have heard the noise, because he looked over just as they reached the bottom of the pyramid steps.

"Hungry?" he asked, stepping onto the path.

"I woke up late and kinda skipped breakfast," Grace admitted. "I guess my stomach just realized I've neglected it. I'm pretty sure the translation of that was, 'A banana does not a day's caloric intake make.'"

Spence smiled. "That's not good. We need to get you some food." He glanced around. "There was a little restaurant near the entrance. Let's go rustle you up something."

"I can go by myself. You probably want to keep exploring." Grace found herself torn—part of her wanted to spend more time with Spence, but she didn't want to be a burden either.

"It's okay. I could use something too. Then I'll come back and explore more." He gestured in the direction of the visitor center, and the two started walking together.

"I could use a chance to sit down," Grace added, hoping her weariness didn't show too much.

"Walking this place is definitely a workout. But wow—so worth it." Spence shook his head, still marveling at what they had just seen. "It's amazing, you know? That we were standing at the base of something built over a thousand years ago."

"More worth it than any elliptical machine, that's for sure," Grace agreed. "It doesn't even feel real. That something so old, so huge, could still be here..."

They both glanced back over their shoulders as the pyramid disappeared behind the trees. Even in its crumbling form, it felt timeless.

"The stone shows its age," Spence said, "but that's what makes it so impressive. No machinery, no electricity—just pure human grit and ingenuity."

"Can you imagine dragging all those stones into place?" Grace asked. "Let alone stacking them like that?"

"Hard pass," Spence laughed. "I get winded carrying groceries. But seriously, it's wild. When people are really dedicated to something... they can do just about anything."

"Like the early Saints building the Salt Lake Temple," Grace said. "That took, what—forty years? And they still kept going."

"Maybe it was the same for the Maya," Spence said thoughtfully. "Different beliefs, different cultures—but the desire to build something sacred? That seems universal."

They walked in silence for a few minutes, each lost in thought. Around them, tourists chattered and children darted between their parents, but Grace and Spence hardly noticed. Grace's stomach growled again, more insistent this time. She was ready to eat. Spence was still thinking about the day, marveling at how incredible it had already been—and how much more there was to come.

He stole a glance at Grace from the corner of his eye. Her red hair glinted in the sunlight, and he noticed a light dusting of freckles across her cheeks. He wasn't sure when he'd stopped thinking of her as just another cruise passenger. He wanted to get to know her better. Maybe even become friends.

Then the thought of Julie flitted through his mind, quick and sharp. He looked away, pushing the ache down before it could rise again. He didn't need friends. He didn't need complications.

Except... for the first time in nearly a year, that ache didn't feel quite so strong.

At the entrance to the visitor's center, Spence reached out and pulled the door open. Grace blinked in surprise. She wasn't used to people opening doors for her. It wasn't that she minded it—she wasn't one of those "I don't need a man" types—but it wasn't something that happened often in her life.

"Oh... thank you," she said, a little surprised by how soft her voice sounded.

"You're welcome," Spence replied, just as quietly.

Chapter 22

Grace's mouth was watering before she even saw the restaurant. The smell of warm tortillas, spices, and grilled meats wafted through the air like a savory siren song.

Spence grinned. "I think your stomach is trying to lead the way."

"I think it's staging a rebellion," Grace whispered back. "And unless we feed it soon, we may have a full mutiny on our hands."

They passed a burger stand, and Grace slowed reflexively.

Spence nudged her with his elbow. "Seriously? We're in Mexico and you're considering a cheeseburger?"

"I mean... it's a classic," she teased. "But okay, okay—you're right. When in Chichén Itzá..."

Spence gestured toward a smaller food stall tucked under a thatched roof. "Let's try something local. You game?"

"As long as it doesn't involve chili peppers and animal organs, sure. I really don't handle spicy foods that well."

He chuckled. "So instead you'd go for a jalapeño burger? I think you're risking your tongue no matter where we go."

"That's fair. But I'd rather not have hallucinations of serpent gods because I ate something too spicy or otherwise cursed!"

They stepped up to the stand, grabbed a pair of menus, and slid into a shady seat near the edge of the courtyard.

Spence flipped his open and made a face. "It's official—I have no idea what any of this means."

Grace studied hers and smirked. "I recognize... two words. One of them is pollo. The other is taco. That's it. We're doomed. I think I'm only fluent in Taco Bell Spanish. Nothing on here says chalupa!"

"This is where we need McKay. He actually knows Spanish from his mission." He leaned in conspiratorially. "We could do the 'close your eyes and point' thing. Menu roulette. You up for an adventure?"

"You go first," Grace said, raising an eyebrow. "I want to know what kind of food karma you have before I commit to something like that."

"Fine." Spence shut his eyes dramatically and stabbed his finger at the menu. He peeked. "Poc Chuc. That sounds intense. Probably something that bites back."

"Or just chicken. Everything mysterious is always chicken," Grace said, amused. "All right, my turn." She closed her eyes, wiggled her finger like a game show contestant, and dropped it.

"Pollo Pibil," she read aloud. "I have no idea what that is either."

Spence chuckled. "Great. Mystery meat times two. We'll either survive or bond over shared trauma."

"Hey," she grinned, "this might be a highlight of the scrapbook. 'That time we blindly ordered lunch and hoped for the best.'"

"So, what's the over-under on one of us crying from spice?"

Grace tapped her chin thoughtfully. "I'd say sixty-forty. I cry, you steal my lunch, we call it even."

"Well, if I start speaking in the ancient Maya language, all bets are off." Spence winked.

"Oh no. If that happens, I'm out. You're on your own. I'm not dealing with any sort of Montezuma's revenge that ends in spiritual possession."

Their laughter bubbled up again, and this time, it didn't just fill the space—it settled into it. For the first time in a long time, neither was thinking about the pain their exes caused.

Chapter 23

The waiter arrived with a polite smile, pen poised. "Ready to order?"

Spence nodded confidently. "Sí. I'll have the Poc Chuc."

Grace hesitated, then pointed to her choice. "Pollo Pibil... please. Is it spicy?"

"Not too spicy," the waiter assured her with a warm grin. "Very flavorful. Slow-roasted. You'll like it."

Spence grinned. "She's spice-sensitive. Thinks black pepper is an act of war."

Grace kicked him lightly under the table.

"And to drink?" the waiter asked.

Spence started to answer, but the man interjected, "I recommend the agua de piña. Pineapple water. Very refreshing. Made fresh this morning."

Spence looked at Grace. "What do you think? Want to try it?"

Grace bit her lip. "Pineapple water? Is that... safe? It's not like, tap water, right?"

The waiter laughed. "No, no. It's purified. Fruit water. Very clean. Sweet and cold."

"Sounds perfect," Spence said. "We'll take a pitcher."

As the waiter walked away, Grace raised an eyebrow. "Are you sure that was a good idea? I've always heard you shouldn't drink the water in Mexico."

"Don't worry so much. I saw plenty of people drinking water when we walked in. And the waiter made it sound like this is totally normal. Tourist-tested." Spence tried to sound confident, though his voice wavered slightly.

Grace narrowed her eyes. "What have you gotten me into? You know there's no natural freshwater here, right? The Mayans used cenotes and rain collection. What if that's what this is?"

"They're not out back scooping puddles into glasses," Spence assured her. "We're in the twenty-first century. I'm sure they import or filter everything now. I even saw bottled water near the gift shop."

Grace sighed. "Well, I suppose it has to be better than that lemon water they always serve at Relief Society functions. I swear it tastes like sadness and tap."

Spence crinkled his nose. "I've always wondered about that. Is the lemon supposed to mask the weird aftertaste? Or is it part of the punishment?"

"I've never figured it out. I always bring my own bottle and hope no one notices. Don't tell—I'll probably be shunned."

Spence mimicked her and placed a finger to his lips. "It's our secret. I won't tell."

"Good, because I've seriously considered bringing sugar packets to make lemonade. One day I'm going to do it."

"Next ward dinner, I'm bringing sugar," Spence whispered. "Operation Lemonade Rebellion."

They were still giggling when the waiter returned with a tall, frosty pitcher and two glasses. He poured generously, then left with a nod.

Grace eyed the liquid. "It looks a bit... frothy."

"At least there aren't giant pineapple chunks floating in it. That's already a win compared to lemon water." Spence lifted his glass. "Well, no time like the present. Bottoms up."

He drank, then gave a surprised nod. Grace watched him closely—no choking, no possession, no spontaneous conversions to Mayan mythology. She took a small sip.

"Oh—wow," she said, surprised. "That's actually good. Sweet, but not too sweet. I may have just found my new go-to drink."

Spence took another sip. "I'm ruined. I'll never be able to drink lemon water again."

Grace's eyes sparkled. "You know what? I think I just figured it out!"

Spence looked intrigued. "Figured what out?"

"The story behind the lemon water."

"Oh, this I have to hear."

"Okay," she said, gesturing dramatically, "totally conjecture here, but just go with me. The people who built this place? Descendants of Nephi, right?"

"Sure. I'm with you."

"And you know how there are those lost pages of the Book of Mormon?" Grace leaned in conspiratorially.

Spence nodded solemnly. "The ones Martin Harris lost."

"Exactly. So clearly, on those lost pages, there was a divine fruit water recipe. But Joseph lost the pages... so now, no recipe."

Spence fought a grin. "So what you're saying is... somewhere on those pages it said, 'And it came to pass that verily I say unto you, mix the sacred juice of the pineapple with cold water, that it may bring strength and wisdom.'"

"YES! But it was super detaily, you know how scriptures are."

"Detaily?" Spence laughed. "Is that a word?"

"Shush, I'm testifying here!" Grace grinned. "Anyway, it was probably all about tablespoons and cubits."

"Right—how many tablespoons in a cubit?"

They both burst out laughing.

"But!" Grace continued, "Emma's trying to host Relief Society, and she knows Joseph mentioned this divine fruit water. Only, they can't find pineapples anywhere in Kirtland, so she substitutes lemons."

Spence nodded gravely. "And thus, lemon water was born."

"Exactly. And it's stuck ever since."

They both wiped their eyes, still laughing, just as the waiter returned with their food. The aroma silenced them mid-giggle. Their plates looked colorful, strange... and delicious.

Spence leaned forward. "So, what do you think?"

Grace poked her fork at the roasted chicken wrapped in banana leaf. "It looks like nothing I've ever had before."

"That could be good, right? You came for adventure. You got adventure."

"I thought the pyramid was enough adventure," she said. "Now I'm supposed to eat something I can't pronounce?"

"Let me guess, Pollo Pibil isn't Taco Bell approved?"

Grace laughed. "Definitely not on the dollar menu."

She took a deep breath and tried a bite. She chewed slowly, then blinked. "Wow. It's citrusy... but garlicky too? And not spicy at all."

Spence smiled. "That's a win. Let me try."

She offered him a bite, and he nodded in agreement. "That's actually really good."

"Your turn." She pointed to his plate. "Let's see if you got the cursed dish."

He cut a bite and chewed thoughtfully. "Also delicious. We might have just discovered the secret to divine lunch ordering."

"Faith, randomness, and pineapple water." Grace raised her glass and grinned. "To adventure."

Spence clinked his glass to hers. "To pineapple prophecy."

Chapter 24

"I think I ate too much," Grace moaned as the two left the little restaurant.

Spence chuckled. "Let's walk it off. Want to check out the visitor center while we digest?"

Grace nodded, grateful for a break before more outdoor sightseeing.

They headed toward the gift shops clustered near the entrance to a small museum. Spence gestured toward the museum, and Grace gave a thumbs-up.

Colorful stalls displayed painted pottery, woven textiles, and carved animals. Grace made a mental note to return and buy something for Aaron. She smiled, picturing her son's messy toy chest and mischievous grin. Normally when he stayed with his dad, she missed him—but this time it felt different. He wasn't just across town. He was in a whole different country.

"Penny for your thoughts?" Spence asked gently.

"Oh... I was just thinking I should get something for my son. But he's so spoiled, I don't know what. He really doesn't need anything," she said with a grin.

Spence smiled, but the remark hit a tender place. He thought about picking up small trinkets for his nieces and nephews, but it wasn't the same. Still, for the first time since Julie left, he allowed himself to imagine having a family again.

It surprised him.

For nearly a year, he'd been stuck in survival mode. Work, Church, repeat. He hadn't realized how heavy his heart had become until it started to lift.

Grace didn't seem to notice the shift in his expression. They stepped into the museum together, and the quiet atmosphere wrapped around them like a blanket.

The exhibits were small but impressive: cracked bowls, smoothed tools, delicate jewelry—relics of lives long past. Grace stood before a chipped clay bowl, marveling at the intricacy of the pattern. "It's so detailed. And it's still here after all this time."

"Wow, look at this," Spence whispered reverently from the next display. He stood beside a case filled with weapons: chipped spears, stone blades, and what looked like a heavy ceremonial sword.

Grace joined him. "I guess that's not your bow, Nephi. It's not broken."

Spence ignored the jest, his eyes locked on the sword. "Can you imagine? Wielding something like this in battle, like in the Book of Mormon. The Nephites against the Lamanites..."

His eyes went distant, as though he could see past the glass to the world that once was.

Grace glanced at the sword again. "It's huge. And I can't help but think about where they mention in the Book of Mormon about beating their swords in to plowshares. I can't imagine."

Spence reached toward the case before stopping himself. "Like when Nephi went back to get the plates and ended up fighting Laban. It must've been so hard, but he did what he had to do." He mimed holding the sword. "Take that, Laban!"

Grace blushed as several museum-goers looked over. "Hey, Spence, calm down. You're starting to sound like my son. Now put your sword away before someone calls security."

"Fine," Spence said, grinning as he lowered his imaginary weapon. "But I bet Nephi's mom never stopped him."

"Maybe not. But I'm not her. And I'd rather not explain to the embassy how you accidentally stabbed a tourist with a ghost sword."

Spence laughed, still captivated. "Seriously though... can you imagine crafting that without power tools? We can't get a DVD player to last six months, and they made this by hand—and it's still around."

"Maybe because it wasn't mass-produced in a factory overseas," Grace joked. "Built to last."

"Exactly."

They walked through the rest of the museum, pointing out favorite items and tossing playful theories back and forth.

"You know," Spence said, "I love reading about the Book of Mormon and all, but I don't think I'd want to live in that time. Don't tell McKay. Might ruin his image of me."

Grace laughed. "What, afraid you'll lose your street cred with the young crowd?"

"Absolutely. The family reputation is at stake here."

"Oh no, national security!" she teased. "What now, Agent Nephi?"

Spence struck a mock heroic pose. "It's top secret. If I told you, I'd have to... well..."

"Kill me?" Grace raised an eyebrow. "OK, 007. Calm down. I'll keep your cover. You're macho Nephi-man, ready to launch your time machine back to 550 BC."

Spence nodded solemnly. "Exactly. Now... for wardrobe. Think this outfit works?" He pointed to a mannequin dressed in replica Mesoamerican garb.

Grace studied it. "Maybe. But I think we need to age it a bit. You want to blend in, not look like a theme park extra."

He grinned. "Fair point. Want to coordinate? You could wear that one." He pointed to the female mannequin.

Grace tilted her head. "Mmm... not sure that's my color. Do they have it in red? And where's the price tag?"

"See, customer service just isn't what it used to be," Spence said with a wink.

They both broke into laughter, their voices echoing through the quiet halls. When they exited the museum into the bright afternoon sun, Grace checked her watch.

"We only have a couple hours left. Anything else you want to see?"

"What about your son's souvenir?" Spence asked.

"I'll grab something in town if we run out of time. I really want to take in as much as I can before we have to leave."

"If you're sure. I'll help you remember," Spence offered as they stepped back into the sun.

"It's hard. He's only seven. Most of this stuff would just break or not mean anything to him."

"Doesn't make you a bad mom," Spence said gently.

"I know. It's just... you want to get it right. He's into Transformers, Legos, army guys, and racecars. Not a lot of that here."

Spence grinned. "What about a t-shirt? 'My mom visited a pyramid in Mexico and all I got was this dumb t-shirt.'"

Grace burst out laughing. "He'd probably love that! Too bad I didn't see one!"

She gave him a playful punch.

"Ow. First the drink spill, then you trip and tackle me, now this. I think you're trying to take me out."

"I'm really not trying to be a walking disaster," she said softly. "I'm just... a little clumsy."

Spence smiled, brushing it off. "I'll survive. Besides, how much more damage can you do?"

Grace raised an eyebrow. "You might not want to ask that."

Chapter 25

The map said they stood in The Ball Court. Spence and Grace looked around. The field stretched for forty yards and was flanked by two twenty-five-foot stone walls. Vertical stone hoops were set into the walls, weathered by time but still imposing.

"So... it's a field. And they played ball here?" Grace asked, eyebrows raised. "Men are all the same. Doesn't matter what century—give them a ball, and they'll find a way to make a sport out of it."

Spence looked toward a stone structure at the southern end of the court and pointed. "Hey, maybe that's the locker room."

Grace squinted against the sun. "I don't know... I still haven't seen one of those freaky water things. If that's the bathhouse, I'm passing."

"Look at these carvings," Spence said, walking over to one wall and crouching beside it. The weather-worn stone depicted graphic scenes of warriors and sacrificial rituals tied to the ancient game once played on the field.

Grace joined him and frowned at the imagery. "So what the heck is this—soccer meets basketball meets horror film?"

"It does look intense. Seems they played with a ball you couldn't touch with your hands or feet—maybe hips or elbows?" Spence looked up at the stone hoops far above. "And those are easily twenty feet high. Imagine scoring that goal."

"Yeah, and it looks as bloody as a hockey brawl. Is that guy missing a head?" Grace pointed to a particularly grisly carving.

Spence squinted. "Yup. That's definitely decapitation."

"Okay, that's enough ancient ESPN for me. Let's move on," Grace said, stepping quickly out of the court.

"How about the Group of the Thousand Columns next?" Spence asked, consulting the map.

"That was on my list! Let's go."

As they made their way in comfortable silence, the Temple of the Jaguars loomed into view. Grace paused to photograph one of the sculpted jaguars perched near the entrance, adjusting her camera to frame the shot just right.

"There's a lot here. It's all so fascinating," Spence said. "The more we see, the more amazed I get. I know I keep saying that, but it's true."

"I'm the same way. In my head I just keep repeating, 'This is amazing, I can't believe this.' I'm getting tired of my own inner monologue!" Grace laughed as she slipped her camera back into its case.

Spence nodded. "What gets me is thinking about the scale of it all. No cranes, no bulldozers. Just sheer will."

"I'm glad we're both too dorky to come up with better words for it," Grace joked.

"Right? But honestly, being here feels like standing in a dream. Like when I went to the Grand Canyon—it was so big and surreal, my brain didn't fully register it as real."

Grace's brow furrowed. "What do you mean?"

"It just felt impossible. Like my brain kept saying, 'Nope, this can't be a real thing.' Most of the stuff I see at home in Richmond is modern. But this?" He swept his hand around them. "This is ancient. It's hard to wrap your head around."

"Well, I've got proof you were here," Grace said, holding up her camera. "Photos or it didn't happen."

"Are these the friends who tricked you onto this cruise?" Spence asked with a smirk.

"The very same. I might need you to vouch for me—I doubt they'll believe I really climbed a pyramid!"

"I've got your back."

Chapter 26

"OK, it's a deal. I'll give you some of my pictures so you can have your own proof," Grace said.

"You've certainly taken enough today. You must have spares to share. Do you really like photography that much?"

Grace beamed. "Oh yeah. I figure the more pictures I take, the better chance I'll get a few good ones. My boss at the camera store asked me to bring some back for display. I'm supposed to make a photo book, too. And my friend at the craft store wants a few scrapbook pages."

"So your job is making you work on your vacation?" Spence teased.

Grace laughed. "Basically. But it's the part I love. I started scrapbooking in eighth grade and never stopped. Before my divorce, I lived in the craft store. I even worked there part-time when Aaron was in preschool. When I had to go full-time, the manager helped me get hired at the camera shop next door."

"But you still make things for the craft store?" Spence asked.

"Sometimes. They always need display pages. And I've got plenty of prints. I think my family's tired of getting scrapbook layouts as gifts, though," Grace said with a smirk.

Spence chuckled. "I've always admired creative people. Me? I used to lose my film rolls in a kitchen drawer. I finally switched to digital, but even then I just upload the photos and forget them."

"That's a tragedy. All those poor memories sitting on a hard drive." Grace mock-gasped. "You've got to promise me you'll print at least one picture from today. Something that reminds you how happy you've looked all day."

Spence smiled softly. "All right, I promise. One photo, printed and framed. But how do I pick?"

"Find the one that speaks to you. The one that tells your story of this place."

Spence nodded. "I'll take your expert advice."

They walked slowly toward the path leading to the cenote. "So," Spence asked, "you've been taking photos a long time?"

"My grams gave me my first camera. But I got serious about it my senior year. I was one of the yearbook photographers. I've just always loved it."

"I was a swimmer. That was my thing," Spence said. "Actually got scouted once for the Olympics."

Grace's eyes widened. "No way!"

He laughed. "I didn't make the team. But I did get to meet some really cool people."

They reached another gift shop near the visitor's center, just before the trail to the cenote. Grace pulled out the map. "This must be the sacred water site. Wanna check it out?"

Spence raised a brow. "Sure. Sacred, water, mysterious sinkhole... What's not to love?"

The two approached the edge of the cenote, its limestone walls curving down to the green-tinged water far below. A plaque explained how the Mayans relied on it as a freshwater source, and archaeologists believed it had ceremonial significance—possibly even human sacrifices.

Grace stared into the murky depths. "So this is where they got their water? I don't even see a pulley system or anything."

"Maybe they lowered buckets on ropes. Or maybe someone climbed down?" Spence guessed.

"Ugh. I wouldn't bathe in that, let alone drink it."

"Come on, be brave. We'll get a rope and a pail. You first," Spence teased.

Grace shot him a glare. "You're lucky I don't throw you in."

"If you do, I'm dragging you with me. We can reenact ancient Mayan rituals together."

Grace peered down again and shuddered. "No thanks. I'll stick to city water from here on out. Chlorine has never sounded so good."

They shared a laugh, turned from the cenote, and continued down the path toward the columns—still full of energy, discovery, and the quiet, surprising ease of each other's company.

Chapter 27

"Grace, I have to say it," Spence looked at the expanse of stone columns before them.

"Say what?"

"I can't believe this. It's so..." He started.

They finished together, "Amazing!"

Spence grinned at her. "I can't believe you knew what I was thinking! It's a... a... miracle!"

"Yeah right," she chortled. "Only cause we've both said it what? A zillion times today?"

"I know. We're so sad. I went to college. You'd think I would have a better vocabulary." He shook his head.

"New plan. When we get back to the States, we invest in a word-a-day calendar. Right? Then the next time we see something like this, we won't be amazed. We won't say it's amazing. We'll say something like," Grace paused to think. "Um... impressive! Yeah! This place is so impressive!"

"Exactly! We'll go somewhere outstanding. We will be astounded. We'll look at remarkable sites and see... great... I can't think of anything else... I think I'm back to amazing." Spence frowned. "Yup, totally pitiful."

"Word-a-day calendars it is, then. We'll be like walking dictionaries! Thesauruses even!" Grace declared.

"Not only that—our friends will be amazed at the amazing words coming from our amazing vocabularies! It'll be completely amazing!"

"I see you are on the same amazing wavelength that I am on," Grace said. The two could not help but laugh at themselves. They were both educated, articulate people, but the sights of Chichén Itzá had reduced them to simple exclamations of awe.

They stood in front of The Thousand Columns. The complex held the Temple of Warriors, surrounded by tall, wide stone columns that once may have supported a thatched roof. Now, they reached skyward on their own—silent sentinels in stone.

Grace stood in the shade of one of the columns, fanning herself with her hand. "At least it's kinda shady here."

"Yeah, maybe that was the whole point. Imagine this place in the dead of summer—scorcher. Maybe this was their version of a shaded hangout," Spence mused.

"I'd bet you're not far off. Beating the heat had to be brutal. I swear by my air conditioning. If I lived in a place like this, I'd have melted into a puddle!"

"Women today. So spoiled by modern conveniences," Spence shook his head in mock chagrin.

"Watch it, buster. I am spoiled, and I like my modern-day wonders. Air conditioning, bottled water, microwaves—divinely inspired, all of them!"

"There's nothing wrong with that. Honestly, I do too. I've gotten soft."

"Soft? Please. You were ready to climb a pyramid! You've walked around here like it was nothing. I'm practically dying. You haven't even broken a sweat," Grace said, a little impressed.

"I still swim and stuff, but that's not what I meant. I just meant that when I was a kid, I'd go camping all the time, do all kinds of crazy stuff. Now? I don't want to sleep in anything but a real bed in a real hotel."

"I feel that. These days, the Howard Johnson is roughing it," Grace joked.

Spence laughed. "That's fair. Of course, now I can't help but wonder what you think about this trip."

Grace wiped sweat from her brow. "Well, my friends kind of bought my ticket and kidnapped me. But honestly? This cruise ship is the opposite of roughing it. A girl could get used to that kind of lifestyle."

"So you want to live on a cruise ship now?"

Blanching at the thought of never escaping Megs' bubbly commentary, Grace shook her head. "Uh, no thanks. I'll keep my feet on dry land."

Spence's grin grew. "If that's what you wanna call it—'grounded.'"

Grace was adamant. "Yes. Grounded. I'm just a simple North Carolina girl. I wouldn't want to get confused and become hoity-toity. Better to go home to my little apartment, my son, and my photo lab job. It's the simple life for me!"

"Well, if you insist. Though I still think you'd make an excellent professional cruise-goer."

"Sure. Right after I invent a portable scrapbook studio and figure out how to beam it to the ship."

"You know what? That actually sounds like a real business plan," Spence said as he ducked behind one of the pillars.

Grace's eyes narrowed. "You'd better run."

Chapter 28

Spence darted between the columns, laughing as Grace gave chase. She lunged around one of the massive stone pillars, but her sandal slid on the stone path and she skidded sideways. Her hand smacked against the rough surface with a loud thwack.

"Ouch!" she exclaimed, cradling her knuckles.

Spence popped out from behind a pillar, his grin vanishing the moment he saw her. "Are you okay?"

She flexed her fingers, inspecting the scraped skin. "I think so. Just a few battle wounds."

"You're racking them up this trip," he teased gently. "We'll have to stop by the ship's medic later. See if you can get patched up with some fancy cruise ship Neosporin."

Grace sighed. "I usually carry little packets of that stuff. But thanks to Paige and her 'vacation makeover,' I have nothing useful."

"Okay, I need to ask—what's the deal with Paige and your stuff?"

Grace rolled her eyes. "She threw me out of my own bedroom and packed my bags herself. Said I wasn't allowed to be antisocial and hide with my books and t-shirts. She wanted me to look human and act, you know... sociable."

Spence laughed. "What were you trying to pack?"

"Comfortable clothes. My stack of six novels. Some snacks. Stuff to make the trip bearable. Paige decided I needed cute outfits and forced socialization."

"Sounds... familiar," Spence said. "McKay did the same thing. Told me I wasn't allowed to hide behind my Book of Mormon. He wanted me to 'get out there.'"

Grace tilted her head. "You think our friends' ideas of fun are different from ours?"

"I know they are," Spence replied softly.

They both paused. The silence lingered just a little too long. Grace's heart did a small flip, and she glanced away, brushing a stray hair from her face. She didn't know what to say—but she also didn't want to say goodbye just yet.

They made their way back toward the heart of Chichén Itzá. Beneath the trees, vendors had spread blankets covered in colorful souvenirs. A barefoot girl with long black braids ran toward them, her small box of gum held out with hope in her eyes.

"Chicklet? Chicklet?" she asked, waving the box up toward them.

Spence knelt down and examined the offerings. "Grace, what do you think? Spearmint or fruit punch?"

Grace wrinkled her nose. "I hate chicklets, but... oh no, she's cute."

Spence pulled out some pesos and bought two little packs, handing one to Grace and tucking the other into his pocket.

The little girl skipped back to her blanket and handed the coins to her parents. Spence smiled after her, then slipped a piece of gum into his mouth.

Almost instantly, he grimaced.

Grace arched an eyebrow. "Well?"

He lowered his voice. "I forgot how nasty these things are."

"Then why'd you buy them?"

"She was adorable. I'm a sucker. I admit it."

Grace softened. "I get it. I'm the sucker in my apartment complex. I buy every fundraiser item kids bring to my door. Even the nasty popcorn."

Spence pointed to a nearby trash can and walked over to discreetly dispose of the gum. "I do the same at my office. My patients' kids bring me junk. I have a closet full of stale candy and popcorn."

"I hoard mine till Christmas and use it as emergency gifts. Mostly for people I don't like."

Spence mock-gasped. "You re-gift popcorn?"

"Only the really bad flavors."

He looked thoughtful. "I'm a dentist. If I start handing out candy and popcorn... that's job security, right?"

Grace burst out laughing. "You're terrible!"

"Terrible, but strategic," he said, rubbing his hands together in mock villainy. "Together we'll take over the world... one molar at a time."

"Evil genius dentist strikes again!" Grace was laughing so hard she had to wipe tears from her eyes.

As their laughter died down, the sun dipped lower in the sky. There was something different in the air between them now. A little lighter. A little warmer.

Neither one said it aloud, but they both felt it.

Something had shifted.

Something good.

Chapter 29

We've got half an hour before we have to board the ship again. I'm going to see if I can find something for Aaron. You're more than welcome to join me... if you want." Grace hoped she sounded casual. After the day they'd had, she honestly hoped he would.

Spence blinked, caught off guard. His palms suddenly felt clammy. "I... uh... I... sure."

Just behind them, McKay rolled his eyes and winked at the redheaded girl he'd been talking to. "I think I'm heading down to the beach before we get back on the ship. You two have fun, though."

"But we only just caught back up with you—" Spence started, but McKay had already turned and gone.

Grace laughed. "How do you even keep up with him regularly?"

"Sometimes I don't even bother," Spence said, sighing. "He's always been like this. A mile a minute in every direction." He gave her a small smile. "So... want to start browsing? Any idea what you might get?"

"Still no clue. But I'm sure something will jump out at me. Maybe one of those maraca thingies. Then Aaron can drive me up the wall with the noise."

"Aww, he wouldn't really do that to you, would he?"

"Oh yeah, he would. But I'd still let him. I miss that little rascal."

"Let's find him something, then. Maybe it'll help take your mind off missing him so much." Spence's gentle words warmed her heart.

They wandered through a stall bursting with color and texture, falling into a comfortable quiet. Grace absently picked up a painted wooden burro, trying to picture whether Aaron would like it. A sudden tap on her shoulder made her spin—and burst out laughing so hard she snorted.

Spence stood there wearing the world's most obnoxious striped poncho and a massive sombrero. "How about the native look?" he asked with mock solemnity.

Grace clutched her side, gasping. "You look like a cartoon! Oh, this is a miracle. I can't even breathe!"

"I believe Aaron needs the entire outfit," Spence said, striking a pose. "What do you think?"

Grace wiped tears of laughter from her eyes. "It's a bit big for him, don't you think? I mean... it fits you!"

"I didn't say it'd fit perfectly. Just that he needs it." Spence looked mock-offended. "Besides, maybe they have smaller sizes."

"You need to buy that for yourself. It suits you." She tried to contain her laughter, but the grin was impossible to hide.

"Yeah, and where would I wear it?"

"Halloween! You'd make a fantastic Pablo the Evil Dentist. Handing out toothbrushes to kids while looking like a giant piñata."

"I'll even hand out my business cards. Double threat."

Grace smirked. "You're the superhero no kid wants to meet."

Spence waggled a finger at her. "Truth, justice, and good dental hygiene."

"Well then, you'd better buy it. Meanwhile, something like that probably would make Aaron happy. He'd totally love the crazy colors."

They rifled through the stack until Grace found a smaller poncho in green and orange. "He'd like this one. And it'll only drag for three or four growth spurts. What do you think?"

"Great colors. Rock on."

"Oh, if we're doing this, then he definitely needs this hat." Spence thrust an eye-searing, multicolored sombrero into her hands.

Grace winced. "Is there a color not on this hat? It's hideous. He'll love it."

She started to ask the price when Spence suddenly grabbed her arm. "Wait. If I have to wear this, and Aaron's getting one, you have to match us. It's only fair."

Grace froze. "No. Absolutely not."

"C'mon. Trick-or-treating mom-and-son outfit. You'll look amazing."

"I'll look like a walking fruit salad. No way."

But Spence was relentless. He plopped the hat on her head, triumphant.

"I—I don't think so!" she sputtered, hands full.

"Too late!" he grinned. He quickly bartered with the vendor and handed over cash.

"All sales final," the vendor declared with a wink.

Grace turned on Spence, torn between annoyance and amusement. "You did not just buy this."

"Grace, give in. It's okay. Really."

"At least tell me what I owe you. And I am not wearing that on Halloween."

But Spence suddenly looked uncertain, rubbing the back of his neck. "I... I'm sorry. I didn't mean to overstep. We can figure it out later..."

Her irritation vanished. Grace gently set down Aaron's items, took the poncho, and threw it over her shoulders. Then she added the hat with theatrical flair. "All right. You win. Aaron would think this is the coolest thing ever."

Spence blinked, stunned. "You look great. It... really suits you."

Grace shifted Aaron's things to one hand and, on impulse, reached out with her other hand to lightly touch Spence's arm. She leaned in and gave him a quick hug. "Thank you. For helping me shop. For everything today. Really."

She turned and started walking toward the ship, leaving Spence standing there, stunned.

It took him several seconds to recover—and then he followed, still feeling the warmth of her hug, and the chaos she had quietly brought into his heart.

Chapter 30

"She did? And you're complaining, why?" McKay looked over a forkful of creamy pasta at his cousin.

Spence rubbed his forehead and sighed. "I just don't know where it came from. And... I don't know..." Grateful that McKay was seriously listening instead of being his usual goofball self, Spence wondered if there was any hope of making sense of the day's events.

McKay didn't know what his cousin wanted to hear. "Why does it have to mean anything? Maybe you should chill. It sounds like you and Grace had a nice day. You joked around. You actually relaxed. You checked out some wicked cool places. Maybe that's all it was."

Spence took a long swallow of ice water before responding. "You're probably right. It probably meant nothing but... you... I—"

McKay set down his fork. "I'm sorry I mess with you so much. I know Julie was a downright wench. She trampled you for no good reason. It takes time to get over that. I know you say you're not looking for anything, and that's okay. But it also sounds like Grace isn't looking for anything either. You know how girls are. They're just more... touchy-feely."

Spence sighed and stared at his plate. "Thanks. I do know you understand. I'm really glad you came home when you did. I honestly don't know what I'd have done this past year without you. You kept me going. I know I whine, but like this cruise? I'd never have done anything like this if you hadn't pushed me."

"I just hate what Julie did to you. But listen—you really do need to move on. Yes, that's easier said than done, but you deserve to live again. Every time you have a chance, she crops back up in your head. Stop letting her have that control."

"I just don't know how," Spence admitted quietly. "But I really did have fun with Grace. That hasn't happened in a long time." His smile was weak, but it was genuine.

McKay cleared his throat to mask the urge to cheer. "Then maybe you should talk to her again. There's nothing wrong with hanging out with her on the cruise. Why pass up on more fun? Just because you hang out doesn't mean you have to date her or marry her. You could really use a friend."

"But what am I supposed to say? 'Gee, Grace, I think you're swell—but let's keep it platonic and no more of that hugging nonsense'?" Spence rolled his eyes. "I don't think so, McKay."

McKay sighed. This was going to take a while. "No, don't go acting like a loser. Just walk up to her. Tell her you had fun and thought you might enjoy hanging out again tomorrow. Keep it simple. Stop overthinking everything."

"And what if she brings up the hug?"

"Cuz, don't even mention it. Let it slide. It's good, okay? It's not like she tried to jump your bones. Just assume it was friendly. That's how girls are."

"You're right. I should relax." Spence leaned back and looked at the ceiling. "You know... I never did have an easy time with girls. Not like you. I kind of envy that."

"Envy me? What for?"

"Because you make it seem so easy. I had all those sisters back home, and I still don't understand women. I was never comfortable with the whole dating scene. Why do you think I barely dated before... before Julie?"

McKay chuckled. "I've seen you with women. You're a dork. But that's the new cool. Chicks dig it. You're golden—whenever you feel like reentering society. For now, just go with the flow."

Spence looked doubtful. "And if Grace brings up—"

"She won't," McKay cut him off smoothly. "And even if she did, who cares? Let's say you two do a little flirting. It's a cruise. You never have to see her again after this week. It's harmless. Could even do you some good. But frankly, I doubt it'll even come up."

He picked his fork back up. "Now. You up for some dessert, or what?"

Spence groaned, rolling his eyes. "Food and women. Women and food. You think of nothing else."

McKay grinned wickedly. "So that's a yes to dessert... and a maybe to women?"

Spence tried not to smile. "We'll start with dessert."

Chapter 31

Grace rummaged through her scattered clothes and luggage in search of her flip-flops. Surely Paige hadn't removed those, too. What was she supposed to wear to the pool—heels? She searched again, moving things two or three times, but came up empty.

"I give up," she muttered under her breath, grabbing the least complicated pair of sandals she could find. Who knew a nighttime swim could be such a hassle? At least she still had a decent swimsuit—no telling what Paige would've picked out if given the chance.

With a towel slung over her shoulder and a magazine in hand, Grace slipped out of the cabin and headed toward the upper deck. The exhaustion in her bones was undeniable. She hoped the pool would help ease the tension lingering in every muscle.

As she made her way to an empty deck chair, Grace reflected on the day. It wasn't something she could forget—her sore legs reminded her with every step—but it wasn't just the physical fatigue that overwhelmed her. It was everything.

Her life was a steady rhythm of early mornings, school drop-offs, work shifts, dinnertime routines, and bedtime stories. There was never enough sleep, and always more to do. But she loved it. The simple, predictable rhythm brought her comfort.

On days off, she and Aaron would find little adventures—day trips to Raleigh, Chapel Hill, or Durham. Museums, parks, science centers. They were lucky to live in such a culturally rich area. Still, those excursions couldn't compare to wandering among the ruins of the Yucatán. Grace never imagined herself seeing ancient civilizations firsthand. She was just a single mom from North Carolina.

And then, there was Spence.

She wasn't sure what to make of that yet. Today had been unexpectedly... good. He was funny. He was kind. He was easy to be around. It wasn't about looks or flirting—it wasn't even romantic. It was just easy. Comfortable. Familiar.

She smiled to herself, realizing what it was. She missed having guy friends. Growing up, she'd always had them. She'd never been a tea-party girl—she climbed trees and raced bikes. As she got older, those boys became young men at school and church, and they stayed her friends. But after getting married, that shifted. It wasn't appropriate to have male friends anymore, not the way it had been. And after her divorce... well, it just hadn't come up.

But with Spence, it felt like coming home to something she hadn't realized she'd missed. He reminded her of those days—of feeling accepted for who she was without needing to impress anyone. She hadn't expected to connect with someone like him. She definitely hadn't expected to enjoy it so much.

They had parted ways when they returned to the ship. Spence went to find McKay. She'd gone back to her cabin to drop off her purchases. She found herself wishing they'd made plans to meet again tomorrow.

The pool water was perfect—cool enough to refresh, warm enough to soothe. The sea air drifted gently across the deck as Grace eased into the water, each stroke slow and lazy. Floating under the stars, she felt a rare and precious peace.

Life was hard. That would never change. But she wouldn't trade it for anything. Grace never planned to be a single parent—it just happened. Her Aunt Macy had shown her what that kind of life looked like, and how strong a woman had to be to make it work. Grace admired that. And like Aunt

Macy, she carried the weight without complaint, doing her best for her son every single day.

This cruise had been a gift—literally and figuratively. She would never have afforded it on her own. Her friends knew she needed it more than she did. She had resisted, but now she saw the truth: coming on this trip was one of the best decisions she'd ever made.

For the first time in a long time, she felt it—relaxed. Fully, genuinely relaxed. And it felt good.

Grace reached the edge of the pool and pulled herself out, her legs dangling in the water as she sat on the rim. She leaned back, eyes closed, letting the salt-kissed breeze play over her skin as the day replayed in her mind.

The laughter. The connection. The ease of it all.

That was what she wanted more of in her life—days that didn't feel like survival, but living. She didn't know how to make that happen. There were still bills to pay, lunches to pack, routines to follow. But just for now, she let herself forget all that. Forget tomorrow. Forget what waited at home.

For now, she would breathe. And smile. And remember that somewhere in the middle of ancient ruins, bad sandals, and fruit water, she had found something she hadn't felt in a long time.

Hope.

Chapter 32

Spence woke with a start as McKay's pillow collided with his face.

"What the heck do you think you're doing?" he groaned, peeling the pillow off his head.

McKay stood grinning like a lunatic. "Hey grumbly sleepyhead, wake up! I want to get to breakfast early. We didn't get enough time to eat yesterday."

Spence rolled over, eyes squeezed shut in protest. "No way. You forget how old I am. My mission was about a billion years ago. I feel no need to arise at dawn just to eat, you freak."

McKay chuckled. "It's all you can eat, man. Come on. I'm a growing boy."

Cracking one eye open, Spence mumbled, "Yeah, you'll be growing all right. But I don't think you're gonna like the bigger waistband."

McKay struck a dramatic pose and flexed his biceps. "Not with my workout routine. I'm gonna always be a hottie. Now get your butt in gear. Or do you not care about that trip to Tulum after all?"

That got Spence's attention. He tossed back the covers and swung his legs out of bed. He used to think like McKay—invincible, energetic, borderline obnoxious—but time had a way of humbling a man. His body now reminded him he wasn't twenty-one anymore. Workouts weren't just optional tune-ups. They were survival.

Still, Tulum. The second day of tours. Just thinking about it sent a bolt of excitement through his chest. He'd been dreaming of this site for years. A fortress city perched against the sea. It wasn't hard to imagine Nephite warriors defending the walls, Lamanite scouts lurking in the jungle. It stirred something inside him.

"Hey, McKay," Spence called, rifling through his clothes. "Did you know Tulum is one of the most visited archaeological sites in the entire Caribbean? Imagine—all those tourists walking around, totally unaware that the people who built that city worshipped Jesus Christ."

McKay was halfway to the bathroom. "Uh-huh. Cool story, bro. You gonna be the tour guide today?"

"You laugh, but I bet you've learned more already than you thought you would."

Through the door, Spence could barely make out McKay's muttered reply. "Only 'cause you won't shut up, dude."

Spence smiled as he shook out a shirt and slid it over his head. He wasn't even offended. Truth was, it felt good to care again. To feel excited about something other than work or callings. He hadn't expected this trip to mean anything, but something was shifting.

Maybe it was the adventure. Maybe it was Grace.

That thought gave him pause.

Grace.

Yesterday had surprised him more than he could admit. He hadn't planned on anyone tugging at the tightly wound cord he kept around his heart, and yet she had—softly, unexpectedly. Her warmth. Her laughter. That moment in the market.

And then... the hug.

He felt his ears heat up just thinking about it.

It wasn't a romantic moment—not exactly—but it had meant something. It had felt real. And terrifying. And... good.

"Yeah well," he called out as he pounded on the bathroom door, "sue me for trying to help your testimony grow. You about done in there?"

"Hold your horses! For someone who slept in, you're sure in a rush."

Spence smirked. He could hear the sink running and the rustle of McKay's routine behind the door. He was glad he'd showered and shaved the night before. Gave him time to pull himself together before the day began.

As he laced up his shoes, Spence looked toward the balcony. The sun was rising—gold light bleeding across the sea.

It was going to be another unforgettable day.

And for the first time in a very long time, Spence felt ready for it.

Chapter 33

"Like, wow. This is the best cruise ever! I just can't believe how beautiful everything is! And did I tell you about how I met four guys yesterday? I like totally love the Caribbean!"

Grace barely heard her roommate's bubbly remarks. Instead, she focused on her day bag, double-checking its contents to make sure nothing important was missing.

"Uh-huh," she mumbled, tucking in a few extra rolls of film.

"So there was Mark, and he just got home from a mission in Bangkok, Thailand. Did you know they're not even allowed to proselyte there? He said he didn't have a single baptism his entire two years, but that he wouldn't trade it for anything. Isn't that amazing? He really got the spirit of missionary work. And—get this—he made me try a mango! I don't think I've ever eaten a mango before. It was like... wow. Really good."

Grace considered the weight of her camera, the last thing to go in the bag. She had toyed with the idea of converting to digital photography for months. It would be faster, easier, and cheaper in the long run. But there was something about film—something tangible. Slower, yes. But real. Like the kind of memories you developed, not just clicked.

"Uh-huh," she said again, almost automatically.

"And then there was Jacob—he's studying to be an oncologist. That's a cancer doctor, you know? He had this mission companion who survived leukemia as a kid, and it totally changed his outlook on life. He was telling me all about how this guy's spirit just lit up everyone around him, even though he'd gone through something so awful. Like, can you imagine?"

Grace closed her bag and stood. "Yeah, I guess. Hey, I think I'm gonna head out early. I decided I want to go on that day trip. I hear the view's beautiful, and I'd love to get some photos while the light's good."

Megs looked genuinely baffled. "Seriously? That's all you can think about? Photographs? What about... all the men? Have you even really looked for a man this week?"

Grace sighed. "Megs, I have a child. Dating isn't that simple for me. I came on this cruise to unwind, not to husband-hunt."

Megs sputtered. "What? But at least have some fun! Enjoy the eye candy! I mean, a little harmless flirting never hurt anyone. What about that guy you disappeared with yesterday—what's his name?"

Grace swallowed. "Spence," she said softly. "We had a fun time. The sights were just..." She trailed off, then smiled. "Amazing."

Megs squealed. "See? I knew it. Love is in the air! You and Spence—you're so made for each other. Look at that smile! You've only known him for like five seconds and already—"

"What? No. It's not like that." Grace shook her head, scrambling to find the right words. "It was just... the day was great. He's... nice. That's all."

"Oh, sure. If you're not engaged by the end of this cruise, I bet you'll at least be an item," Megs said dreamily. "Hey, wait up!"

But Grace was already out the door, walking briskly down the hallway, hoping the momentum would carry her past the heat creeping up her cheeks.

"Grace!" Megs called, adjusting her purse and hurrying after her. "I said wait up!"

Grace didn't slow down.

She had photographs to take. Light to chase.

And just maybe... someone to run into.

Chapter 34

"I'm so glad we're going to the beach, cuz."

Spence glanced at McKay. "Are you kidding me? The beach? That's what you're excited about?"

"Uh, yeah! It's the beach. In the Caribbean. Think of the water, the relaxing—and the babes!" McKay adjusted the towel slung over his shoulder like it was a trophy.

"You're seriously going to skip the ruins at Tulum for the beach? There's actual archaeological evidence that—maybe even the Three Nephites—"

"Yeah, yeah, moldy-oldy blah de blah," McKay interrupted. "I'm here for sun, fun, and female companionship. You really ought to hang out with me. We could—"

Spence held up a hand. "How many times do I have to say this?"

"No, no how many times—you just need to relax. Have fun. Stop being a nerd. This is a Mormon cruise, not a pilgrimage. Build your testimony about girls again. It's fine. No one expects you to be Peter Priesthood 24/7. They just want to see you."

Spence groaned. "Did you really just say no how many times?"

"Don't change the subject. Girls, Spence. That's where it's at. Even the prophet would forgive you. He's married, after all."

Spence exhaled slowly. "I'm not trying to impress anyone. I just... care about this stuff. The Book of Mormon sites. The history. That's what I came for."

And, truthfully, it was why he'd made sure to avoid Grace that morning. He'd spotted her boarding another ferry, bound for the same location. He'd ducked onto a different boat.

All because of one hug.

Which was ridiculous. It wasn't a kiss. People hugged all the time. It didn't mean anything. Still, it had rattled him.

He shook off the thought and checked his camera—again. Battery full, memory card ready. Today, he would focus. No distractions. Just history.

"Earth to Spence." McKay's voice cut through the spiral of thoughts. "Where'd you go?"

"What?"

"We're almost there. I asked if you were gonna be looking for Grace, but you were off in la-la Spence land."

"I'm not looking for Grace. I'm going straight to the ruins."

"You should talk to her. You two seemed pretty chummy yesterday. This is the perfect chance to—"

"To what? I already said—"

"Stop! You're being no fun. Listen hard, because I'm only saying this once. I don't even care if you like Grace. Just be decent. If you see her—talk to her."

"For what—?"

"Did I say stop? Don't make me double dog dare you."

Spence rolled his eyes. "Are we twelve again?"

"Nope. But just listen, okay?" McKay's tone turned serious for once. "Talking to a woman won't kill you. Talking to a woman doesn't mean you're picking out rings. It's a conversation. That's it. Forget Julie. Forget work. Forget all of it. Just for the rest of this cruise—be the guy you were before all of that happened. Remember? You were fun once. Don't you remember what fun is?"

Spence was ready with a snarky comeback... until he wasn't.

Because McKay had a point.

Sure, Spence did "fun" things—basketball with the guys, working out, diving into books—but he hadn't felt fun in a long time. Not really. Yesterday might've been the first time in ages he'd smiled and meant it.

"You're right," Spence said quietly. "I know I haven't been much fun."

"Yeah, no kidding," McKay muttered. "Look, shut the door on all that for now. You can pick it back up when you get home if you want. But right now? You're on vacation."

McKay practically pronounced it in all caps.

"Fine. I'll pretend nothing awful has ever happened. Happy now?"

"Almost." McKay leaned in. "If a girl says hi, you don't run. You don't make it weird. You talk. Like a human. Not a wounded monk."

"Will it get you to shut up?"

"Only about this," McKay grinned, flashing his perfect teeth.

Spence sighed again. "Fine. I'll talk to people."

"Women. You will not hermit yourself into obscurity."

"Fine. No Hermit-Spence."

"Progress!" McKay beamed. "Honestly, I think you and Grace had a spark. If she can handle your rambling gospel history lessons, she might just be worth sticking around. Because me? I'm hitting the beach. There's probably someone waiting for the McKay-meister to make her Caribbean dreams come true."

Spence shook his head. "You're a lunatic."

"You're just jealous of my tan," McKay called as they disembarked.

Spence slung his bag over his shoulder and glanced toward the path ahead. Somewhere out there were sacred ruins. Somewhere out there was Grace.

And maybe—if McKay was right—something more.

Chapter 35

Grace boarded the bus bound for the ruins of Tulum, camera in hand and a buzz of anticipation tingling through her. She couldn't wait to photograph the legendary view—those ancient ruins rising above the bright blue Caribbean. This wasn't just any beachside snapshot. This was a dream setting for a scrapbook page, something beyond patterned paper and stickers from the craft store. Nothing she brought with her could compete with what nature—and history—were about to hand her.

She clutched her beloved Canon SLR, the one she saved up for so painstakingly after the divorce. Before everything fell apart, she'd eyed it as a luxury. Now, it was a symbol of taking something back for herself. Her mother's words still echoed in her ears: "Grace, you deserve something. Do it for you."

And she had. Despite the twinge of mom-guilt every time she thought of the price tag, she'd done it. And she'd learned so much. Understanding aperture, shutter speed, and lighting made her look at the world differently—more thoughtfully, more creatively. Her friends noticed. Her customers noticed. The first time someone asked for her advice, she almost laughed in disbelief. "I'm just a girl with a camera," she'd said, but deep down, it felt good to be taken seriously.

This trip to Tulum? It was her reward. She planned every angle. She even researched vantage points in advance. All she needed now was good light—and maybe a little luck.

She looked up from her camera settings and spotted McKay and Spence through the window. The two seemed to be parting ways—McKay toward the beach, Spence toward the bus. She quickly shifted in her seat and fiddled with her bag, suddenly self-conscious. Should she offer him a seat? Would it seem too eager?

When Spence stepped onto the bus, she risked a smile, hoping it wasn't too obvious. He met her gaze, and for a moment, hesitated. Then, slowly, he approached.

"Is, um, anyone sitting here?" he asked.

"No. You can join me." Her voice came out calm and neutral. Hopefully. Inside, she was flustered.

"Um... thanks." Spence sat, his camera already hanging around his neck.

She glanced at it. "Are you going to actually use it today?"

"What?" Spence blinked.

"Your camera. You had it yesterday, but didn't take many pictures."

"Oh. Um. Yeah. That's the plan..."

He sounded off. Grace studied his expression—tired, distant. Not what she expected after his passionate enthusiasm the day before.

"Are you OK?"

He exhaled. "No. Well. Yes. I mean... I don't know. McKay and I got into an argument. I didn't sleep well. You know. Life."

Grace nodded. "I get it. My roommate practically gave me a migraine before I even left the room. She's at the beach now. Lucky me."

He grunted. "Ain't that the truth."

The bus engine rumbled to life, and as they pulled away, Grace noticed Spence finally relax a little.

"You know," he said, "I am excited. This site might be even better than Chichén Itzá."

"Really? That was a pretty amazing place. Is it the ocean view?"

He chuckled. "No, though McKay would definitely say yes."

Grace laughed with him. "Same with Megs. Though she's more interested in rings than ruins. I feel bad for any guy trying to enjoy the beach."

Spence groaned. "Don't even get me started on how obsessed people are with marriage."

Grace's smile faded. "Well, yeah. That's probably because they've never been married."

The bus grew quiet. The words hung awkwardly between them.

"I'm sorry," Grace said quickly. "I don't know why I said that."

"No, it's all right. I get it. Not every marriage is sweet and nice."

Grace nodded. "Sometimes I get frustrated. I had this dream of what it would be like... and it just wasn't. But everyone still expects me to be chasing the fairytale."

"I know what you mean," Spence said. "Being divorced in the Church is like wearing a sticker that says 'damaged goods.' No one wants to talk about it, but it's there."

Grace looked at him, her voice soft. "You're not alone."

Spence offered a weak smile. "Thanks. That actually helps. Doesn't make me feel any less like I've been stamped 'rejected,' but... yeah. Thanks."

"Well, we're not like McKay and Megs. At least we can be thankful for that," she said with a grin.

Spence laughed. "Amen to that."

Chapter 36

"What are you looking forward to most?" Grace asked, sensing the shift in his mood.

Spence lit up. "What aren't I looking forward to? There are two different temples here. Did you know on April sixth, you can see Venus shining straight through the doorway of one of them?"

Grace's eyes widened. "Seriously?"

"Dead serious. It's incredible. The alignment only happens on that day. The precision is unreal. They say it's tied to the birth of Christ."

"That's wild. How did the Mayans even know how to do that? I can't figure out half the constellations with an app, let alone build something that lines up with a star."

"Right? They didn't have computers. No telescopes. Just the night sky and a deep sense of purpose."

"And you think it's connected to Christ?" she asked, fascinated now.

Spence nodded. "Think about it. The Nephites would've known those dates. Oral traditions are powerful. Combine that with astronomical tracking? It's possible they passed it on, even without the written records we lost."

Grace sat quietly, awestruck. "You know... I love the Savior. But I don't think I've ever shown that in a way like this. Not with carvings or buildings or... stars."

"Same. I mean, we have scripture study and prayer. But building a temple with a celestial alignment? That's devotion."

Grace shivered—not from cold, but from something deeper. "And to think Joseph Smith chose April sixth to organize the Church... and this place wasn't even re-discovered until years later."

"Exactly," Spence whispered. "It gives me chills. People want to say Joseph made things up, but there's so much he couldn't have known. Not back then."

She smiled. "You're really passionate about this."

"I guess I am. It just makes everything feel... more connected."

Grace looked out the window and saw the turquoise water beyond the cliffside. "We really did come at the wrong time of year."

Spence laughed. "I've already thought that. Maybe next time, we come back for the equinox and April sixth."

Grace sighed. "That would be amazing. Maybe in another lifetime."

He grinned. "Well, I hear heaven has great group rates."

They both laughed, and Grace could feel the shift—their conversation no longer about sadness or regret, but about awe. About faith. About wonder.

Spence adjusted the camera strap around his neck. "So, what are you hoping to capture today?"

Grace looked down at her SLR and smiled. "Something that makes people stop and feel something. Not just a pretty picture—but something that makes them think. Something... sacred."

Spence nodded, his voice quiet. "That's what I want, too."

As the bus pulled up to the edge of the ruins, Grace's heart beat faster—not just for the photos she might take or the history she might uncover, but for the sense of wonder she hadn't felt in a long time. Maybe this was more than a trip.

Maybe it was the start of something new.

Chapter 37

"Okay, so here's the first thing that really fascinated me when I was studying the early teachings of Joseph Smith," Spence began, his voice filled with reverence. "Did you know he once said Zion's ancient name was Zama?"

Grace shaded her eyes from the harsh Caribbean sunlight and looked up at the Temple of the Descending God. "Zama? Can't say I've heard that. What's the big deal?"

Spence gestured toward the weathered stone temple. "Zama is what this place—Tulum—was once called. But the name wasn't rediscovered until the twentieth century. That, and the whole April sixth Venus alignment thing? That didn't become known until way later, either."

"But you said Tulum was discovered in the 1800s?" Grace asked, tilting her head.

"The site was known, yeah. But the full significance—the way the sun and Venus align through the temple's doorway on April sixth? That wasn't discovered until someone just happened to be standing here on that day." Spence's eyes sparkled. "And Joseph Smith named April sixth as Christ's birthday nearly a century before anyone knew what this temple did."

Grace let out a low whistle. "That's kind of wild. Like, what are the odds?"

"Right?" Spence grinned. "So you've got this site called Zama—Zion—this astronomical event tied to the founding day of the Church... It's one of those things that gives me chills."

Grace nodded slowly. "Okay. I'm not saying I believe in coincidences, but if I did..."

Spence laughed. "Exactly. And to the Mayans, birthdays were a big deal. They tracked celestial events like crazy, and every god had a birthdate. When you realize how precise they were with astronomy, it kind of makes you think—how much did they really know?"

She tilted her head thoughtfully. "That's actually kind of beautiful. And weird. But beautiful."

Spence hesitated, then added, "It's almost like April sixth was their way of remembering the birth of Christ—long after He visited them."

"That's..." Grace trailed off, her voice quieter now. "Wow."

They stood in companionable silence, surrounded by stone and sunlight and the hush of ancient memory.

Grace squinted up at the carving over the doorway. "So, what exactly am I looking at again?"

"That," Spence said, pointing, "is the Descending God. He's carved upside down—feet in the air, head first toward earth."

Grace raised an eyebrow. "I'm sorry, but... it kinda looks like a baby being born."

Spence choked on a laugh. "I wasn't going to say it, but... you're not wrong."

She giggled. "Well, hey, I guess it fits. If they built this whole thing around a birthday."

Still chuckling, Spence watched as she unzipped her bag and swapped lenses on her camera. The way she moved—focused, graceful, in her element—captivated him. Sunlight caught the coppery streaks in her curls, and something stirred in his chest. Not romance exactly, not yet—but something tender and true.

Without thinking, he lifted his own camera and snapped a photo.

Click.

Grace lowered her camera and blinked at him. "Did you just take a picture of me?"

Spence froze. "I... yeah. I guess I did. Sorry. It's just... you looked really happy. Like you were in your element. I thought maybe you'd want to remember that."

There was a pause. Then, to his surprise, Grace's expression softened. "Thanks. That's actually... kind of sweet."

Spence looked down at his camera, suddenly self-conscious. "You ready to see the rest of it?"

"Absolutely," she said with a smile. "You promised me more history, Professor."

Chapter 38

As they walked around to the next structure, Spence pointed toward another weathered temple. "Okay, this one might be even more interesting."

Grace shaded her eyes again. "Do I get more Mayan trivia?"

"You do," he said proudly. "See those three doorways? The center one has another carving of the Descending God."

"Seriously? That guy shows up a lot," Grace said, raising her camera again.

"Yeah. Now look to the left." He pointed carefully. "That doorway has a carving some believe represents the Descending God's father."

Grace's eyebrows lifted. "So... like Heavenly Father and Christ?"

Spence nodded. "Exactly. And the third doorway?" He paused. "It's blank. No carving at all. Some scholars think that's intentional—meant to represent the Holy Ghost. No form. No image."

Grace stood quietly for a moment, absorbing it. "That's... kind of brilliant."

"Right? And the thing is, these people were dismissed as 'heathens' for centuries. But here they are, echoing the very structure of the Godhead."

"They remembered pieces," Grace murmured. "They may have lost the details, but they remembered the heart of it."

Spence glanced at her, surprised by how closely her thoughts echoed his own.

Grace sighed. "I came here thinking I'd get a few pretty shots for the scrapbook store. This is way deeper than I expected."

Spence nodded toward the ocean. "And look at that view."

Grace turned toward the ocean, where turquoise waves shimmered against the crumbling edges of history. "This. This is the picture I want. The temple, the sea... it's like stepping into a story."

Spence watched as she carefully framed the shot. "This site—it hits different, doesn't it? Not just history. Something more."

"Yeah. It feels sacred," Grace said softly. "Like you can breathe here in a way you can't back home. It's not just history. It's... connection."

"To what?" he asked.

She hesitated. "To everything. To something bigger than me. To God, maybe. And to... I don't know. Peace."

Spence didn't respond right away. He stood still, letting the weight of the place settle over him. The steady hush of waves below mingled with the quiet presence of the ruins. Something stirred in his chest—a memory, a longing, a whisper of faith not lost, just sleeping.

Nephi had always been his hero. Brave. Devoted. Faithful when it counted. And now, surrounded by the architecture of a people who may have descended from that legacy, he felt the stories come alive—not in his head, but in his heart.

He looked at Grace again, the sunlight curling through her hair as she raised her camera. For a second, he saw not just the woman before him, but the shared awe between them— this strange, sacred wonder of finding something meaningful amid ancient stone and shifting sand.

For the first time in a long while, Spence felt something like peace.

Not just because of the scriptures.

Not just because of the sea.

But because for the first time, he wasn't alone in it.

In that moment, he silently thanked Nephi—not just for building ships and cities in the scriptures, but maybe, just maybe, for building a bridge back to his own heart.

Grace snapped another photo, then turned and smiled at him. "So. What's next, Professor?"

And with the soft echo of her laughter trailing behind them, they walked side by side deeper into the sacred city—two hearts learning, slowly, to believe again.

Chapter 39

"May I be of assistance?"

The voice—gently accented and warm—startled Grace and Spence. They turned to find a lean man with smile lines creasing his face and a glint in his dark eyes.

"I am Tameron, a local guide here at Tulum," he said, clasping his hands in front of him. "I give short walking tours to visitors. Perhaps I can share a few things you might not discover on your own?"

Spence looked at Grace, eyebrows raised. She gave a small shrug. It might be nice to hear more than what he'd read online.

"Sure," Spence said. "We'd love that."

Tameron smiled and gestured for them to follow. "I grew up not far from here," he explained as they walked. "Started giving tours at sixteen to save for school. Now I only come back during summer breaks, but this place... it still speaks to me."

They rounded a corner of the great fortress temple and joined a small group gathered at the cliff's edge. The ocean sparkled below like a field of gemstones.

"Friends," Tameron called out, "let's begin by introducing ourselves."

A bubbly voice piped up from the left. "Hi, ya'll! I'm Missy from Dallas. This is my first cruise ever—and oh my heck, is it amazing! Is anyone else here Mormon?"

A well-dressed woman with a sleek bob offered a polite smile. "Not me. I'm Leah, visiting while my husband's at a conference. The hotel concierge recommended this."

Spence cleared his throat. "I'm Spence, and this is Grace. We're on the same cruise as Missy, I think. I'm from Virginia and love this kind of historical stuff."

"I'm from North Carolina," Grace added. "Mostly I just came for the view and to take photos. This is my first time leaving the States, actually."

"Are you a photographer?" Missy asked eagerly.

"Oh no. I just work at a camera store. It's more of a hobby."

Two guys introduced themselves next—Chase and Wayne, friends from Portland on vacation.

Tameron clapped his hands. "Excellent. Now we're all friends. Let us explore together."

As they walked toward the next site, Missy dropped into step beside them. "So, are you guys having fun on the cruise?"

Grace gave a small smile. "More than I expected. My friends surprised me with the ticket."

"They must love you a lot."

"They're also all married. I think that's why they sent me. Married people love to play matchmaker."

"Tell me about it." Spence muttered.

Missy glanced at him. "You're married?"

"Was," Spence said shortly.

The abruptness made Grace wince. He hadn't sounded that sharp before. Hoping to ease the tension, she chimed in. "I'm divorced too. And I have a son. That's why this trip felt... impossible, honestly."

Missy nodded. "Breakups are rough. I've had my share, but I guess it's easier when there are no kids and no papers involved. I joined the Church last year, and this cruise felt like a chance to connect—with God, with the scriptures, with people."

Spence's expression softened. "That's kind of why I came, too. The history, especially. Just thinking about these ancient cities... the possibility that Nephi or Samuel the Lamanite might've walked right here. It gives me chills."

"I know!" Missy beamed. "I wanted to stand where they might've stood. Not everyone gets that."

As the group approached a smaller, low temple, Tameron turned and gestured toward it. "This is what we call the Initial Temple. It marks the beginning of the sacred complex. It dates to around the early fifth century. Inside was an altar and, when discovered, a stele—likely used for funerary rites."

Missy tried to peer over the heads of Chase and Wayne and accidentally stumbled, bumping hard into Spence. He caught her instinctively.

"You okay?" he asked.

"I'm fine," she said, her hand lingering on his arm a little longer than necessary.

Grace looked away, pretending to examine the worn edges of the temple's entrance.

Tameron beckoned the group forward again. "Come. The Temple of the Frescoes awaits."

Chapter 40

The group wandered slowly from the fortress temple, the sun now a bit lower in the sky, casting long, golden beams across the ancient city. A soft ocean breeze tugged at Grace's hair as she glanced back over her shoulder at the Temple of the Descending God, its carved façade now partially in shadow.

Tameron's voice rose above the hush of shifting footsteps. "We will now walk toward one of the most famous structures at Tulum—The Temple of the Frescoes."

The path dipped slightly, revealing a smaller, sun-bleached building nestled low against a patch of scrubby greenery. Unlike the towering fortress behind them, this temple felt humble by comparison—close to the earth. Approachable.

Grace slowed her pace, unconsciously aligning her steps with Spence's. The air smelled of salt and stone. Inside the Temple of the Frescoes, time felt thick. She imagined flickering torchlight illuminating the walls, centuries ago. The mood had shifted in the group. Something quieter, more reverent had taken hold.

Spence exhaled deeply. "I've read about this one. The detail here—it's different. More intimate somehow."

Tameron gestured ahead. "This building contains one of the few surviving examples of painted wall murals from this region. We call them frescoes. They are fragile, and you must stay behind the rope, but you'll still be able to see them."

As they approached, Grace caught her breath. Faded pigments clung to the inner walls—ochres, dusky reds, hints of soft blue. The images weren't entirely clear, but the suggestion of human forms and outstretched arms spoke of something purposeful. Sacred, even.

They turned their attention back to Tameron, who explained the temple's frescoes—vivid paintings of deities and symbols, now faded but still potent. "This entire city centers around the Descending God," he said. "He appears again and again, shown diving from the sky."

"Diving?" Grace whispered to Spence.

He smirked. "That's one way to describe it."

Missy perked up. "What are you two talking about?"

"Nothing," Grace said quickly. "Just something funny we noticed earlier."

Spence chimed in, easing the moment. "You'll get it when we circle back to the main temple. It's a visual thing."

"Many believe these frescoes depict local legends," Tameron continued. "But others argue they reflect something more. Stories passed down over centuries—fragmented, maybe. But important."

Grace leaned slightly to the side, trying to glimpse more of the artwork without crossing the boundary rope. "You weren't kidding, Spence. This one really is different."

He nodded. "It almost feels personal. Like we're intruding on something ancient and private."

Tameron pointed out a fresco depicting three men. "These three men seen here are believed to have been important to the region."

"Do they know who the figures represent?" Grace asked.

"There are multiple theories," Tameron said. "Three men, seen in other temples too. Perhaps kings, prophets, or builders. We may not know exactly who they were—but it's clear they impacted the civilization that once lived here in major ways."

Spence looked thoughtful, almost hesitant. "Or... maybe something more."

Grace's gaze flicked to his. "You thinking what I'm thinking?"

He gave her a lopsided smile. "Only if you're thinking about the Three Nephites."

"People say they're still out there," Missy added softly, surprising them both. "After being granted immortality by Christ. Helping strangers. Quiet miracles. Spreading the Gospel. That kind of thing."

"Like spiritual superheroes," Spence said, smiling gently.

They stood for a moment, no one speaking. The sun pressed against their shoulders, and the sea murmured far below. It wasn't doctrine. Not exactly.

But it didn't feel like fiction either.

"Wow," Grace whispered.

Spence nodded slowly. "That would be... something."

Tameron continued, unbothered by the murmured conversation. "The building's western entrance would have allowed light to pour through each evening. Some scholars think the timing of that light was part of a ceremony—or a reminder."

Grace swallowed. "A reminder of what?"

"Of something sacred," Tameron said simply. "Whether it be the sun, a god, or a memory."

Spence stared into the temple's dim interior, lost in thought.

What if it was more than memory? What if these carvings and frescoes weren't remnants of imagination—but echoes of belief? The kind you carried from one generation to the next, even if you forgot the words. Even if you lost the names.

He glanced at Grace. She stood with her arms loosely folded, her camera at her side—not even trying to capture this one.

Some things weren't meant to be framed.

They were meant to be felt.

"I think," she whispered, "somewhere deep down, they knew."

Spence didn't have to ask what she meant.

He just nodded, and they stood quietly together, while ancient light filtered softly through stone and sand.

Chapter 41

The group moved quietly down the dusty path from the Temple of the Frescoes, each person lost in thought. The golden light of late afternoon softened the sharp lines of the ruins, casting long shadows across the worn stone.

Spence walked in silence, his camera forgotten around his neck. He'd always dreamed of walking in the world of the Book of Mormon. But the locations were more symbolic than geographic—legends with uncertain borders. And yet, here he was. At a real place. In a city some believed to be called Zama—Zion.

He kept turning over the thought of those murals. The three men. Could they really be the Three Nephites?

It was the kind of idea people shared in testimony meetings or passed around as folklore—stories about immortal missionaries appearing at car crash scenes or helping stranded hikers change tires in the rain. Never concrete. Always hazy.

And yet, those depictions carved into stone... They felt different. Rooted. Real.

He glanced sideways. Missy walked beside him, still chatty and cheerful. She'd fallen into him back at the altar temple—completely innocent, of course—but the moment had unsettled him. It felt awkward in a way Grace's touch hadn't.

On his other side, Grace walked quietly, camera at her side. Spence found comfort in her presence. It wasn't romantic—he wasn't ready for anything like that—but it was... grounding. She didn't pressure him. She asked good questions. And she got it—the reverence of it all.

He cleared his throat. "Tameron?"

Their guide turned back. "Yes?"

Spence pointed toward the direction they were heading. "Those three figures in the murals... Is there any more information about them?"

Tameron slowed to let the group catch up. "There has been much speculation. Some scholars believe they were seers, spiritual men. Others say they were prophets or even divine beings. They appear in several temples—always as a trio, always central."

Grace leaned in. "Divine beings? Or just important leaders?"

Tameron's mouth curved into a practiced smile. "It depends on who you ask. Some say they were more than mortal. Not gods, exactly, but not entirely human either. Able to perform miracles. Unable to die. Respected across the region."

Spence's heart skipped. Unable to die.

"And what do you believe?" Grace asked, her voice quiet.

Tameron looked at her thoughtfully. "I believe stories are told for a reason. Whether we call them myth or truth, they shape us. And sometimes, I think ancient people knew things we've forgotten."

Grace nodded, her gaze far away.

Spence could hardly contain himself. "That lines up exactly with the Three Nephites. They were granted immortality by Christ—spared from death so they could minister across generations. It would make sense for people to remember something about them, even if it was twisted by time."

Missy, walking a step behind, whispered, "Like spiritual echoes."

He looked at her, surprised. "Yeah. Exactly."

They fell into silence again. The next temple loomed up ahead—low and wide, its roof half-sunken, its painted walls dulled by centuries of sun and storm. The group slowed as Tameron began to explain its symbolism.

But Spence barely heard.

He was still turning over the idea in his head. Not just what if this was real, but what if this mattered?

What if these ruins weren't just historical artifacts? What if they were sacred markers? Proof—not in stone and date—but in continuity. In belief.

His fingers brushed against his camera, but he didn't lift it.

Some things weren't meant to be captured.

Some things were meant to be felt.

Chapter 42

The group paused before the next temple, its once-bright murals now little more than whispers of color. Tameron gestured to the weathered façade.

"This temple is believed to depict elements of creation," he said. "The murals inside are heavily eroded, but you can still see traces of sky, earth, and water. Many scholars believe this was the Mayans' way of honoring the beginning of the world."

Spence leaned forward slightly, intrigued. "You said before that the Descending God represents light and life?"

Tameron nodded. "Yes. In many ways, he was seen as both sun and water. Sustainer and purifier. The source of all things. You can see why the people here built so much around him."

Missy whispered, "Like Christ—the light and the living water."

Tameron didn't miss a beat. "You're not the first to make that connection."

Grace looked at the temple's twelve crumbling steps. "Why twelve?"

Tameron smiled, pleased. "Another debated topic. Some say twelve months of the year. Others point to twelve signs in the zodiac. But religious travelers often tie it to sacred numbers—twelve apostles, twelve tribes, twelve stones."

Spence's voice was thoughtful. "Maybe it was both. Maybe they were remembering something they didn't fully understand, but still felt was important."

Tameron didn't comment, but his eyes lingered on Spence a moment longer than necessary.

Missy nudged Spence's elbow. "You're kinda full of surprises, Professor."

Spence chuckled. "Just a guy with a decent memory and a few too many books under his belt."

Grace smiled to herself. The soft joking, the shared wonder—it felt easy again.

"Here's what fascinates me," Tameron continued. "The western entrance would allow the setting sun to flood the temple each evening. Some believe this was part of a ritual of renewal, or rebirth. The sun disappearing into the earth only to rise again—light overcoming darkness."

"That symbolism shows up everywhere," Spence murmured. "Even in completely unrelated cultures."

"Exactly." Tameron looked pleased. "There is something about light returning that speaks to the soul."

They stood there for a while, letting the quiet settle around them.

Grace glanced over at Spence. "So... do you think this is just cultural overlap? Or something more?"

Spence hesitated. "Honestly? I think people remember what matters. Even when they forget where it came from. Even when it gets all tangled and mixed up. Some truths just... linger."

Missy tilted her head. "Like echoes?"

"Yeah," Spence said laughing. "Like echoes."

Grace looked up at the sun as it dipped lower on the horizon, brushing the ruins in gold. "I'm glad we came today."

Spence didn't say anything. He just nodded—deep, deliberate—and watched the way the sunlight caught the copper in her hair.

Tameron clapped his hands gently to gather the group's attention. "We will visit one more site before we finish. It's not far."

As the others began to move, Missy fell into step beside Spence. "I still can't believe this place. It feels like... like something sacred happened here."

Spence gave her a genuine smile. "Yeah. Maybe it did."

Missy hesitated. "Hey, this might sound random, but—where did you serve your mission?"

Spence blinked. "Australia. Perth Mission. Mandarin-speaking."

Missy stopped short, then lit up. "No way. My brother served there! Mandarin-speaking, same mission."

Spence stared. "Wait—your brother wouldn't happen to be Elder Slintel, would he?"

She clapped a hand over her mouth and laughed. "That's you? You're Spencer 'Professor' Olsen?"

Spence groaned. "Oh no. He told you about the nickname?"

"Only every time you came up. He said you were obsessed with scripture trivia and argued with the Zone Leaders for fun."

"I did not argue for fun—okay, maybe once."

Grace raised an eyebrow. "Wait, wait. You two know each other?"

Spence shook his head. "Her brother and I were mission companions for three months. He talked about you all the time—called you 'Missy-bear,' if I recall."

"Ugh!" Missy made a face. "I hated that nickname."

Grace laughed. "I think it's kind of adorable."

Missy grinned. "I can't wait to tell him I ran into you. He's going to flip."

Tameron turned back toward the group. "Ready to continue?"

Spence gave Missy a mock-bow. "After you, Missy-bear."

"Oh don't start!"

They all laughed, and something warm settled in Grace's chest. This—this laughter, this surprise connection, this spiritual wonder wrapped in real life—that's what she had needed.

Not just a vacation.

Not just peace.

But something real.

And maybe, just maybe, she wasn't the only one.

Chapter 43

The path to the final temple curved along a ridge, giving the group a sweeping view of the turquoise sea far below. Waves sparkled in the late afternoon light, and the breeze carried the scent of salt and sun-warmed stone.

Grace lingered near the back of the group, letting her camera rest against her chest. She didn't feel the need to capture every frame anymore. Some things were better stored in the heart.

Spence had drifted to the edge of the trail, standing just a few feet from the cliffside. He squinted against the light, the wind tugging at his shirt. He looked completely at home and completely lost in thought.

Grace approached slowly. "Penny for your thoughts?"

He startled slightly, then smiled. "Just... thinking about how small we are. And how big this is. Not just the view, but... everything."

She stood beside him, taking it in. "It really is a lot to wrap your head around."

"I keep wondering what Nephi would think if he could see all this now," Spence said quietly. "The cruise ships. The tourists. His people's cities turned to ruins. Would he be sad? Or proud we even remember?"

Grace considered that. "I think... maybe both. But I also think he'd be glad to see people still looking for truth. Even in the ruins."

Spence turned to her, his voice gentler. "Is that what you're doing?"

Grace hesitated. "Maybe. I didn't know that's what I was doing when I got on the boat. But yeah. I think I am."

Their eyes met, and for a moment, the noise of the tour group faded into the sound of the waves.

Missy's voice broke the quiet. "Hey you two! You're gonna miss the last temple!"

Spence laughed. "Coming!"

They caught up with the group, which had gathered in a quiet semicircle around Tameron. The last temple wasn't large or ornate. Its stones were crumbling, half swallowed by time and roots. But it had an undeniable presence—like something still lingered there.

"This," Tameron said, "is thought to have been a priest's residence. Some also call it the Temple of the Wind, because of its position. The locals believe it's sacred ground."

Chase asked, "Why?"

Tameron smiled. "Because when the storms come, the wind howls through this structure like a voice. Some say it's the spirits. Others say it's just physics. But either way, it's earned a reputation."

Grace stepped closer, her voice hushed. "Does anyone still worship here?"

Tameron looked thoughtful. "Not in the way the ancients did. But yes. People still come here. Sometimes to pray. Sometimes to remember. Sometimes to ask for guidance."

Spence pressed his palm against one of the warm stones, reverent. "It's strange, isn't it? How something can be broken and still holy."

Tameron nodded. "The divine doesn't require perfection. It only asks for faith."

Grace felt those words settle somewhere deep in her chest. She wasn't perfect. Her life wasn't either. But maybe—just maybe—she was still whole in the ways that mattered.

As the group began to turn back, Tameron clapped his hands together. "We'll return to the entrance soon. Please stay together. And take one last look if you wish."

Spence and Grace didn't move. Neither did Missy.

Spence's voice was quiet. "I don't know what this place is. Not really. But I feel something."

Missy nodded. "Me too. It's like... peace. But with a pulse."

Grace smiled faintly. "Maybe that's faith."

Spence looked at her, eyes full of something steady and unspoken. "Or maybe it's the start of it."

They didn't need to say anything else.

Together, they turned toward the path, the sun warm at their backs, the ocean calling below, and the wind whispering through the stones behind them.

They didn't know what the rest of the cruise held.

But they were starting to understand what had brought them here.

And maybe—just maybe—that was enough.

Chapter 44

Grace trailed a few steps behind Spence and Missy, letting the buzz of their conversation wash over her like a tide she wasn't quite part of. They were chattering about some elder they both knew—Missy's brother, apparently. The name meant nothing to Grace, but it didn't seem to matter. The two of them had launched straight into a flurry of memories, mission stories, inside jokes.

Grace tried not to bristle. It wasn't their fault. It was one of those things that happened in the Church. Someone dropped a familiar name, and suddenly they were bonded like long-lost cousins at a pioneer family reunion. The six degrees of separation didn't apply in Mormon culture—it was more like two. Maybe one and a half.

Still, something about watching the easy way Spence laughed with Missy tightened in her chest.

She hated how it made her feel—like a third wheel, which was absurd. Spence and Missy had met minutes ago. There was no reason to feel... displaced.

No reason at all.

Except maybe one.

Grace didn't want to admit it, not even to herself, but Spence had a way of getting under her skin—in a good way. A steady, thoughtful presence with a sense of humor that caught her off guard and a kindness that didn't feel performative. He was smart, genuine, and even when he was awkward, he was real.

And real was rare.

Especially as a divorced woman in the Church.

She never expected to find someone on this cruise who actually got it—the sting of loneliness at family-centered activities, the way people offered smiles heavy with pity, the sense that somehow, you were no longer "ideal."

Spence got it.

And now he was laughing with Missy like they'd known each other for years.

Grace sighed and tried to tune out the ache.

It wasn't Missy's fault. Grace liked Missy, actually. She was friendly without being fake. Bubblier than Grace's natural energy but not exhausting the way Megs could be. There was a groundedness to her that Grace hadn't noticed right away, but it was there—beneath the bright smile and the Southern charm.

Still, that connection with Spence. That natural, easy connection.

Grace didn't want to hate her for it.

But she didn't want to let herself disappear, either.

"Grace, you live on the East Coast too, right?" Missy's voice broke through her thoughts, and Grace startled slightly.

"Uh—yeah. North Carolina."

"How big is your ward?"

Grace blinked. "I guess... normal? Not huge. But I live in a decent-sized town."

"Where about?"

"We call it the Triangle. I'm in Chapel Hill—where Duke is."

Missy smiled. "I'm from Dallas, but I actually grew up in a tiny town. Our branch used to meet in a rented building and it took forty-five minutes to get there. I remember passing cow pastures the whole way."

"That's wild. I've never had that kind of drive. My chapel's actually the stake center. Stake conference, youth events... everything happens there."

"What was it like moving east from Utah?" Missy turned to Spence, drawing him back into the conversation.

He shrugged. "Better than Australia. At least Richmond's got plenty of members. It's not Provo, but it's not bad."

Grace grinned. "Didn't BYU have, like, twenty stakes in one zip code? I heard that the Elders Quorum presidency and your roommate could belong to different stakes in the same dorm."

Spence laughed—a full, real laugh that made Grace's stomach do a tiny flip. "Yeah, exactly! It was wild. I don't think I ever saw that many single adults in one place again."

Missy sighed wistfully. "I've always wanted to go to Utah. All those state parks, the mountains, the Church history sites..."

"Oh, it's beautiful," Spence said. "You'd love Arches. I went hiking there once—it was like walking through another world."

Grace absentmindedly ran her fingers over her camera strap. "I've always wanted to go. It's probably never going to happen. Not with Aaron."

Missy turned toward her, tone shifting. "Being a single mom must be hard."

Grace stiffened.

"I guess. But it's my life. I wouldn't trade it. Not for anything."

Missy nodded, surprisingly gentle. "That's amazing. Seriously."

There was no awkward pause, no pity. Just quiet affirmation. Grace found herself softening again.

Spence spoke next, voice lower. "I think the hardest part of my divorce was realizing I'd never have the family I pictured. We talked about kids. I wanted kids. But she... didn't. At least not with me."

Grace felt that pang deep in her chest. "I'm sorry. I can't imagine."

He looked away. "It's probably better. As much as I wish I could've been a dad... I wouldn't have wanted to split custody. Or worse, fight over one."

Grace didn't think. The words came out on their own. "You'd be a great dad."

Spence's eyes met hers, startled.

"I mean it," she added. "I saw the way you looked for stuff for your nieces and nephews. You'd be amazing."

His gaze held hers a beat longer than she expected.

"I hope you're right," he said softly. "Maybe someday. I'd like to believe that."

There was something in the way he said it—quiet, vulnerable, open.

Grace didn't know what he'd been about to say before they were interrupted. But she suddenly wanted to know.

She wanted to keep this connection from slipping away into the Caribbean breeze.

Before she could ask anything more, Tameron raised his hand from ahead. "We'll take a short break by the sea before heading back to the meeting point. Please stay on the path."

Grace fell into step beside Spence, her heart fuller than it had been all day.

Whatever happened next... she wasn't ready to walk away just yet.

Chapter 45

The group gathered once more near the great stone structure known as The Castillo—a massive fortress-temple rising over the cliffside like a silent sentinel.

Tameron lifted a hand. "We are now standing before what many call El Castillo, or 'The Castle.' But this was more than just a stronghold. It was also a sacred place of worship—part temple, part fortress. From up top, you can see the sea. The Mayans could've used this vantage to watch for invaders from land or sea."

He pointed upward. "There are twenty-seven steps leading to the three doorways you see. And as with many Mayan temples, the number may have symbolic meaning—but no one knows for sure. Perhaps, like the twelve steps of the Descending God's temple, these were tied to an astronomical alignment. Or maybe a ritual calendar. But the truth may be lost to time."

Spence stared up at the staircase, a familiar itch tugging at his brain. Twenty-seven. Why did that number matter? He knew he'd come across it somewhere before—maybe in scripture, maybe in his years of trivia-drenched study. It danced on the edge of his memory, refusing to settle into clarity.

He would have to look it up later. Something to puzzle out back on the ship.

Tameron continued, his tone rich with practiced intrigue. "What fascinates anthropologists about this temple is not just the structure, but the symbolism. Above two of the three doors, there are carved depictions—one of the Father of the

Gods, and one of the Descending God. But the third doorway is empty. No carving. No god."

He let the words linger in the warm salt air. "That absence was not a mistake. These people were too precise. Every detail mattered. So why leave one empty?"

Spence exchanged a glance with Grace. They'd discussed this already, standing beneath another temple. The symbolism was too strong to ignore. Three doorways. Two depictions. One left blank.

The Godhead.

It pulsed like a whisper between them.

Tameron nodded slowly, inviting the group into his conclusion. "It is now widely believed that the three doors represent three divine figures—similar to the Christian idea of God the Father, God the Son, and the Holy Ghost."

"But I thought Christians believed they're all one," Leah said, her brow furrowing. "Isn't that the Trinity?"

"Many do," Tameron replied smoothly. "But not all. The concept of the Trinity didn't appear until the third century, at the Council of Nicaea. Even then, not all Christians interpreted it the same way."

"What?" Chase stepped forward, his voice tinged with disbelief. "You're saying not all Christians believe in the Trinity? That's, like... in the Bible."

Spence stepped in gently. "Actually... not quite like that. The Bible says Christ and the Father are one—but it doesn't say they're the same person. It says husband and wife are supposed to become one, too. Doesn't mean they merge into a single being."

He looked to Leah. "You and your husband—do you make all your big decisions together?"

"Usually. Except maybe politics," she said, earning a chuckle from the group.

"But your purpose is shared, right? You want the same things for your family?"

"Of course."

"That's how we see the Godhead. Three distinct beings. United in purpose. Not literally the same person, but fully aligned."

Wayne squinted. "So... not the Trinity. But still working together?"

Spence nodded. "Exactly. Same mission. Different roles."

There was a pause, and then Grace added softly, "It's kind of beautiful, actually. The idea that different beings can still be completely unified."

Tameron smiled. "It is a compelling thought, isn't it? And one that shows up across cultures more often than you'd think."

The group fell into reflective silence, the sea breeze curling around them as if to carry the idea deeper.

Above them, the three doorways remained—two gods etched in stone, and one left blank.

Unseen.

But not forgotten.

Chapter 46

The group lingered beneath the shadow of El Castillo, sunlight warming the worn stone underfoot as Tameron continued, unbothered by the philosophical detour.

"What many do not realize," he said, "is that this building—while spiritual in nature—also had a very practical use. If you placed torches or reflective materials inside the top doorways at night, the light would project far out to sea. It functioned as a kind of ancient lighthouse."

Grace tilted her head. "Seriously? That's incredible."

"Indeed," Tameron said. "This would've helped seafarers avoid the reefs that line the coast and guided them toward shore. Practical and symbolic. A beacon of light. A place of worship. And a defensive stronghold."

Spence's gaze followed the structure upward. "The Mayans really made every stone count."

He found himself thinking about modern life—his condo in Richmond, the drive-thru coffees, the sterile office buildings that all looked the same. This place, though... this place had soul. Function and beauty married together. Even the stairs carried meaning.

Leah seemed to be following a similar train of thought. "They didn't waste a single thing. Meanwhile, we live surrounded by single-use everything."

Tameron nodded. "Affluence often brings excess. The Mayans had to work with what they had. And yet they built things that have lasted for centuries."

"I remember when my husband and I were newly married," Leah said. "He was getting his doctorate, and we lived in a one-room apartment. Every light switch was a debate. We cooked at home, every night. Now? I can't remember the last time I didn't pick up takeout on the way home."

Spence chuckled. "Same here. Dental school wasn't cheap. I lived off of peanut butter, off-brand cereal, and ramen noodles. I still can't smell chicken-flavored ramen without having flashbacks."

Grace smiled. "I remember when we used to search the couch cushions for enough change to buy tacos. Then we'd splurge on delivery pizza when we had a little extra. Now that I'm divorced, I still watch my budget—but it's not quite the same as back then."

Missy nodded, her tone reflective. "My parents always said struggle keeps you grounded. That's probably why the Mayans were so focused. They had to be. When survival takes effort, you don't waste time or resources."

Spence looked up at the temple again. "And they made it all beautiful anyway."

Grace watched him—his brow knit in thought, the sincerity in his voice. She felt that tug again. The pull that said: Don't let this pass you by.

He was kind. Steady. Someone who saw beauty in old things. Who valued meaning, not just ease.

She caught herself wondering what it might be like to hike ruins with him again, somewhere else in the world. Or to show him Aaron's scrapbook from their last trip to the beach. Or to just sit beside him, quietly, without needing to explain her faith or her loneliness.

And then Missy spoke up beside him. "So, what made you pick dentistry?"

Spence turned, smiling a little sheepishly. "Honestly? I liked helping people—and I wanted a job I could do anywhere, even while raising a family. Back when I thought that was how things would turn out."

Grace felt it—a soft, familiar ache. That longing for the life she thought she'd have. And the quiet gratitude for the one she had.

Missy tilted her head. "You'll still have that, Spence. You'd be a great dad. You've got this calm energy that makes people feel safe."

Spence smiled, but something flickered behind his eyes. "Thanks. That's... kind of you."

Grace looked away, focusing on the sea. Missy's words weren't wrong—but Grace had said something similar yesterday. And somehow, it hadn't landed the same.

Or maybe it had.

Maybe that was the problem.

The group started to drift toward the next cluster of ruins, but Spence lingered a moment longer, standing at the foot of El Castillo. Grace watched as he reached up and touched the stone railing—just lightly, as if in reverence.

And then he turned to follow the others.

Grace fell into step beside him. She didn't say anything. She didn't need to.

For now, walking beside him was enough.

Chapter 47

"We're going to be late!" Grace's voice cracked as panic tightened in her chest. Her feet pounded the uneven path, her camera bag thudding against her side. What happens if you miss your cruise ship? Her clothes, her toiletries, her son's souvenir... all of it was back on board. Not to mention her passport.

After the tour, the three of them had wandered the ruins for hours, completely losing track of time. Grace had taken more photos than she could count—especially once Spence let her borrow his digital camera. Free from the constraints of film, she'd gone overboard, capturing every carving, angle, and beam of afternoon light.

They'd been geeking out on Book of Mormon trivia, swapping testimony stories, debating ancient temple meanings. Grace had never felt her faith stretch and deepen the way it had among the stones of Tulum.

But now? Now they were paying the price.

"We'll make it!" Spence called over his shoulder between gasps for air. "Just... run... faster!"

Grace tried, but her side ached and her lungs burned. Missy wheezed beside her, every breath a struggle, but neither of them stopped.

They rounded a corner, and the dock came into view—just in time to see the water taxi's motor chug to life. A few passengers were already on board. The gangplank looked like it had just come up.

Grace pushed herself harder. Please... just a few more seconds...

Spence, a few steps ahead, turned and reached for her. His hand clasped hers firmly, and she felt an unexpected jolt—more than adrenaline, more than urgency. Something electric. Something real.

"Come on!" he shouted, pulling her forward.

She didn't have time to think about what it meant.

She just ran.

They were nearly to the edge when the boat began to shift away from the dock. Spence waved frantically with his free arm. "Wait! We're coming!"

Grace could barely see through the sweat and wind in her face, but she heard the engine slow, then cough into idle. Spence stumbled as he slowed, and she crashed into him. Missy, hot on her heels, barreled into them both, nearly sending all three tumbling into the water.

The driver scowled. "Cutting it a bit close, aren't you?"

Spence laughed breathlessly. "You have no idea."

He offered Grace his hand and helped her into the boat. She accepted it with a shaky smile, her heart racing from more than just exertion. He helped Missy next, as Grace moved to the side to make room.

Part of her wanted to hold onto the feeling of Spence's hand in hers. Another part noticed that he was still thinking of Missy, too—and she hated that she noticed.

Be gracious, she told herself. Don't let something good slip away because of insecurity.

"Missy, sit by me," she said quickly, patting the seat beside her.

Missy flopped down with a groan. "I thought we were gonna be left behind! That would've been a nightmare."

"No kidding," Grace said, tugging her ponytail loose and trying to breathe evenly.

"What happens if you miss the last boat?" Spence asked, leaning forward so they could all talk.

"Not a clue," Grace said. "And I'm glad we didn't find out."

"I think next time I do a day trip, I'm setting like three alarms," Missy said. "Anything to avoid that run of shame."

"Your phone works here?" Grace blinked.

"Sort of. It's an iPhone, but I didn't buy the international plan. So it mostly dies while looking for service."

"Even back home, it's spotty." Spence rolled his eyes. "There are parts of Richmond where I may as well be in a canyon."

"I thought that was just so you wouldn't text and drive," Grace said, catching her breath. "Some of those dead zones feel strategic."

They all laughed.

"In Texas, I'm convinced half the people on the freeway are playing mobile games while eating tacos and doing their taxes," Missy added.

"In the Triangle, they're doing that—plus applying mascara and spilling Starbucks in their laps," Grace said.

"And in Richmond," Spence added with a grin, "they're also yelling at their kids and flicking cigarette butts out the window."

The three of them laughed so hard, Grace had to hold her side.

The man in front of them turned and grinned. "You think that's bad? I swear I saw a woman making a Jell-O salad in her minivan on I-15. Kids in the back were singing Families Can Be Together Forever like it was their last ride on Earth."

Even more laughter erupted.

As the water taxi pulled away from the dock, the breeze picked up, cooling their flushed faces. Grace leaned back, the adrenaline of the near-miss fading, leaving only the glow of shared relief—and something quieter beneath it.

She looked at Spence as he smiled across Missy, their laughter still lingering in the air.

He looked happy.

He looked like someone she wanted to know.

And something in her heart whispered: Don't let this slip past.

Chapter 48

The gangway creaked beneath their feet as Grace, Spence, and Missy boarded the cruise ship, breathless and flushed from the mad dash across the pier. The afternoon sun cast warm light on the water, turning it into rippling gold as the ship prepared to sail once more.

Grace exhaled hard, her chest still tight from the run. She leaned a hand against the railing, heart pounding—not just from exertion, but from the rush of almost missing it all. The boat. The day. The connection.

Missy doubled over beside her, hands on her knees. "Okay... never doing that again."

Spence, trying to look composed but failing thanks to his windblown hair and sweat-darkened collar, gave a dry chuckle. "We're here. That's what counts, right?"

Grace smiled faintly, brushing strands of hair from her face. "Barely."

The trio began to walk slowly down the corridor toward their cabins. The crowd thinned as passengers returned to their routines—pool towels, early dinners, naps in staterooms. The energy shifted again, from frantic to quiet.

"I think I left part of my soul back on the pier," Missy muttered, tugging her bag over her shoulder. "I'm going to go find water and possibly a coma."

Grace paused at a corridor intersection. "Do you want us to come with you?"

Missy shook her head. "Nah. I'll be fine. I'll catch up later—maybe at dinner?"

She gave them both a wave and disappeared into the crowd, her quick steps already fading.

Grace and Spence were left standing in the hushed quiet of the ship's hallway.

The silence between them wasn't awkward—just thoughtful. Full of the weight of a long day, and everything it stirred up.

Grace looked down at her camera bag, then up at Spence. "Thank you... for earlier. For running with me. For helping me not completely fall apart."

Spence looked at her for a beat too long before replying, "You didn't need my help. You just needed someone to remind you you could do it."

Her heart stuttered. His voice was soft. Genuine.

"I still feel like I'm catching my breath," she said.

"Yeah." He laughed gently. "But that's what makes a day like this worth remembering."

Grace nodded, feeling something in her chest tighten in that strange, vulnerable way she'd almost forgotten how to feel. She fiddled with the zipper of her camera bag. "I, uh... I have so many photos from today. More than I expected. And then I kind of went overboard with your camera."

Spence smiled. "Good. That's what it's for."

She hesitated, then added, "Would you want to come with me to the photo lab? I was going to get a few rolls of film printed. Maybe we could go through some of them together?"

His answer was immediate. "Yeah. I'd like that."

They turned together, walking side by side toward the heart of the ship—back to quiet moments, shared memories, and maybe something more waiting to develop.

Chapter 49

"I can't wait to see how the prints turn out." Grace practically bounced beside Spence as they walked the polished corridor of the ship.

He smiled to himself. Her joy was infectious—wide-eyed and genuine, like a kid waiting for a birthday surprise. Spence had mostly suggested they drop off their photos because he was curious to see how his turned out—especially the ones Grace had taken with his camera. Anything had to be better than the blurry shots he usually got.

But the real reason, if he was being honest with himself, was her.

She'd lit up behind the lens. Focused. Centered. It reminded him of how he used to feel when life was simpler—before broken promises and paperwork turned him into someone who second-guessed everything. Watching her work with his camera had stirred something in him he hadn't felt in a long time.

Hope.

And maybe... the quiet beginnings of trust.

He glanced sideways as Grace adjusted her camera bag, still rambling about what she hoped had turned out—angles she loved, colors she tried to catch, fleeting moments she prayed the film had frozen in time. He let her talk. She filled the silence so naturally, it made him feel like the world might still be okay.

At the photo lab, they'd dropped off her film and his media card. The attendant had let them know the prints would take about an hour—but they could request digital copies too.

Spence had nodded and asked for an extra CD. One for him, one for Grace.

It was barely five bucks. But somehow, it felt like something bigger than that.

"An hour's not so bad," Grace said as they stepped back into the hallway. "Long enough to grab dinner and come back after."

Spence nodded. "Sounds like a plan. We can check in with McKay and Megs on the way. I think they're meeting at the usual spot."

Now, as they ambled toward the dining area, he thought about asking if she'd want to borrow the camera again on the next excursion. It seemed only fair. But the thought of inviting her along for something more felt... oddly comfortable.

Almost like it was already a given.

They turned a corner, and Grace craned her neck. "We're supposed to meet everyone here, right?"

"Yeah. McKay texted me earlier to say they were headed this way."

Sure enough, McKay and Megs were already waiting outside the entrance. Megs waved both hands with a grin too wide for someone not on sugar.

"There you are!" McKay called out. "About time—I was starting to gnaw on the railing!"

Spence rolled his eyes. "As if you didn't already eat your body weight at lunch."

"He did!" Megs chimed in. "You should've seen him. It was like watching a documentary on locusts."

McKay gave her a mock bow. "A man has to maintain his energy. Touring the beach takes stamina."

Spence crossed the final few steps and clapped his cousin on the shoulder. "And humility, apparently."

Grace hung back for a moment, then stepped up beside them. "We were waiting for someone else too. Missy was going to meet us."

Spence glanced at his watch. Only about twenty minutes had passed since they'd parted ways at the photo lab. "Let's give it another ten. If she's not here by then, we'll go ahead and get seated."

McKay raised an eyebrow and leaned in with a conspiratorial smirk. "Her? Spence, you sly dog."

Spence groaned. "Oh, come on."

Grace laughed, but it was a touch hesitant. She glanced down the hallway, as if checking for Missy. For a moment, Spence wondered if Grace was nervous too—about what people might think, or maybe about her place in the group.

He suddenly hoped Missy would show up, if only to keep the table from being too lopsided.

It was already five of them now, and on a singles cruise, that was bound to raise eyebrows.

Still, as he stood there with Grace beside him, his cousin cracking jokes, and Megs already halfway through an anecdote about cruise ship trivia games, Spence felt the strangest thing.

He wasn't nervous.

He was looking forward to dinner.

To photos.

To more time with Grace.

And maybe—if he let himself dream just a little—with her standing next to him for more than just one cruise.

Chapter 50

Outside the main dining hall, Grace and Spence spotted Missy waving them down—this time with another woman in tow.

"This is my roommate, Katie," Missy said. "We went to UT together and met in the singles ward our first semester. We've lived together ever since."

Katie was barely five feet tall, with a platinum blonde pixie cut that made her look younger than she was—seventeen at most, though Grace knew better. Her easy smile and confident wave gave her away as someone well past her teen years.

"You're a convert, right?" McKay asked, already slipping into his trademark charm.

Katie nodded. "Yeah, I was baptized just before I left for school. Honestly, I don't know how I would've survived UT without the Gospel. Dorm life can be intense."

Missy grinned. "And if I hadn't met Katie, I'd probably have ended up rooming with Jannie for four years."

"Oh come on," Katie teased. "You loved her."

"She wasn't awful," Missy admitted. "But living with someone who didn't share my standards? Not easy. I'm glad we met. You're like the sister I never had but always wanted."

"Aww." Katie beamed. "So true."

Grace turned toward Missy. "You don't have sisters?"

"Nope. Just seven older brothers. A literal pack of them. I figured once I hit dating age, they'd scare off every guy before my dad even had the chance."

Spence chuckled. "I had the opposite problem. A whole house full of sisters. Good luck getting any bathroom time. And don't even try to use the phone."

As they found their seats, Grace noticed Megs and McKay already deep in conversation. The two were sitting a little closer than necessary, and Grace couldn't help wondering what had gone on at the beach while the rest of them were off exploring ruins.

"So, what did you study in Texas?" Megs asked, seamlessly pulling Katie and Missy into the circle.

"I changed majors three times," Missy confessed. "I started with art, moved to biology—thought I might try marine biology—but math killed me. I ended up with a teaching degree, and now I'm hoping to get hired as an art teacher."

"You were always studying during that bio year," Katie added with a laugh. "I thought you were going to snap and start screaming measurements at people."

Missy groaned. "But hey, that lab partner was cute. What was his name...?"

Katie struck a pose. "Braaaaaaaaad."

Everyone laughed.

"What did I see in him?" Missy asked. "He was such a creep."

"He hit on half the floor," Katie agreed. "Glad you moved on."

McKay leaned forward. "So why not become a full-time artist?"

"I just didn't feel like I had what it takes to make it pro-fessionally," Missy said with a shrug. "Plus, I like food way too much to be a starving artist."

Katie nudged her. "Says the girl who made me gain ten pounds with her experimental pumpkin bread attempts."

"Wait—you baked? At college?" Grace perked up. "That's awesome."

"Technically, yes. But nothing like Katie does. She minored in culinary arts."

"Really?" Spence looked impressed. "That's not something you hear every day."

"It was actually fun," Katie said. "Except for the part where I always had to bring food home. The roommates got spoiled. Anytime I'd come in the apartment they'd be looking for food!"

"Yeah, but you always told us the deal was worth it," Missy cut in.

McKay raised an eyebrow. "What deal?"

"I cook," Katie said. "They clean the bathroom."

"That is genius," Grace said, laughing. "I would've cleaned a hundred bathrooms for good food in college."

"I still can't believe you majored in journalism," Missy said with a smirk. "Such a weird combo."

Grace tilted her head. "That's not that strange. You could totally be a food critic."

Missy grinned. "I'm aiming more for investigative journalism. The Lois Lane type."

"Looking for your Superman?" Megs teased.

"Not exactly. But hey, I wouldn't turn him down if he showed up in a suit and glasses or a cape to save the day."

The group burst into laughter again. Grace relaxed into the easy rhythm of the conversation. She could feel the dynamics shifting—growing more layered, more connected.

"What are you doing now?" Spence asked.

"I got an entry-level position at a paper in Dallas," Missy said. "It's mostly grunt work—covering city council meetings and writing up small community events. Not glamorous, but it's a start."

"Do people actually read those articles?" Grace asked, genuinely curious.

"Oh yeah. People care about weird stuff. I've seen letters to the editor over weather reports and parking meters."

McKay leaned forward and adopted a dramatic tone. "Dear Editor: Wednesday's paper claimed it would be 73 degrees. My thermometer said 72. I demand answers."

Katie choked as she snorted on her drink. "Ow, It burns!"

Spence handed her a napkin. "Dude, you know better than to crack jokes when people are mid-sip."

McKay shrugged. "Hey, I plead innocence."

Grace laughed so hard she had to wipe her eyes. She didn't know if it was the company or just the joy of the moment, but the meal felt like the kind of memory that would stick with her long after the cruise ended.

And maybe, just maybe, the people sitting around her would stick around, too.

Chapter 51

The six of them had fallen into a comfortable camaraderie. Even Megs—who had also joined them at the dinner table, with her open goal of finding a husband—had relaxed in the group dynamic. No one talked about pairing off, no one forced anything, and for Spence, that felt like the biggest relief of all.

For the first time in a long while, he felt himself loosening up around women. No pressure, no expectations. Just real conversation and real laughter.

And full bellies.

"Ohhhhhhhh," Grace groaned, leaning back in her chair. "I think I might need to be rolled out of this restaurant in a wheelchair."

"I know what you mean," Missy groaned beside her. "That chocolate-peanut-butter cake was a personal attack."

Spence laughed. "Yeah, well, I think they'd need a forklift for me. Grace, how are we gonna make it back to the photo lab?"

"You're picking up your pictures tonight?" Missy perked up, her earlier food coma forgotten.

"Yep," Grace said. "Spence talked me into getting prints. Shooting with film, it's kind of like opening a mystery box."

Missy grinned. "Ooooh, like a surprise vacation flashback!"

"Exactly!" Grace echoed. "Except now there's an audience."

"You took pictures of all of us," Missy pointed out. "I wanna see how my hair held up after that windstorm."

"You're welcome to come," Grace offered. "And if there are any you want printed, just let me know."

McKay stretched his arms overhead. "I always like to walk after a big meal. Helps things settle. I'm in. Megs? Katie?"

"Why not?" Megs said brightly. "We've got nothing better to do."

Katie chimed in, "I was thinking about a swim—but I'm not sure my swimsuit fits after tonight's buffet."

McKay winked. "I'm sure it fits just fine. How about we all hit the hot tub instead?"

"That sounds amazing," Missy said. "But Grace, you probably don't want to bring the prints to the pool, right?"

"Not really," Grace said. "I'd rather take them to the room first."

"I've got an idea," Missy said. "Why don't you guys go grab the pictures while we go change? We'll meet back at your suite, look at everything, then head to the hot tub."

Spence nodded enthusiastically. After all the walking they'd done the past couple of days, a soak in the hot tub sounded like perfection. "I'll go with Grace—need to grab my photos too. McKay, can you grab my stuff?"

"Got it," McKay said, already scooting his chair back. "See you at the suite!"

As the group split up, Grace handed out the suite number. When she and Spence were finally alone, the noise and bustle of the dining area fell away, leaving them in the quiet hum of the ship's corridors.

"I'm kind of nervous now," Grace admitted as they walked.

Spence raised an eyebrow. "Nervous? About what?"

"The photos. I mean... I wasn't trying to impress anyone. I just took what looked interesting, and now it feels like I've got this audience."

Spence smiled at the way she chewed on her lip—a little nervous, a little shy. "They're excited because they care. Not because they're judging."

"Maybe," she said softly. "It's just that... no one's ever really shown that much interest in my photos before. Not unless you count my boss—and I'm pretty sure that was just a sales pitch."

"Well," he said, nudging her shoulder, "you're not selling anything tonight. Just sharing. And I think you'll be surprised how much people enjoy them."

Grace gave a small smile, but it didn't quite reach her eyes. "There's one shot I really hope turned out."

Spence felt a tug in his chest at the vulnerability in her voice. "I hope so too," he said quietly. "I want to see it."

And he did. Not just out of curiosity, but out of something deeper. There was something almost sacred about seeing the world through her lens—what she noticed, what she valued, what made her stop and capture a moment.

He wasn't sure how to put it into words. It felt... magical. And important.

Grace nodded. "Guess we'll find out soon."

They fell into silence again, walking side by side. And as they made their way toward the photo lab, Spence realized he wasn't just looking forward to the prints.

He was looking forward to her—and whatever this strange, quiet, wonderful connection between them was becoming.

It was like Christmas morning, and he had no idea what would be inside the box.

He just knew he couldn't wait to open it.

Chapter 52

Grace had completely wimped out at the photo lab. When Spence offered to open his set while she opened hers, she talked him into waiting. She wasn't ready.

Now, standing outside the door of her suite with the sealed envelopes in hand, she wasn't sure if she ever would be.

All her friends back home always said how great her pictures looked, but those were friends and family—people who had to say that. This group? This was different. They were new. Kind. But honest.

She knew her way around a camera, sure. But she had no formal training—just instincts and a lot of hope. Back home, if a photo didn't turn out, she could go back and try again. Not here. Not in Tulum. This was it.

Her hands were shaking as she fumbled with the keycard.

"Are you OK?" Spence took the card gently and swiped it for her.

"What? Oh—yeah." Her voice cracked, and she winced. She tried to laugh it off. "Just... nerves."

Spence's hand paused on the doorknob. "Still nervous?"

She gave a little shrug. "It's silly. I know. Just thinking about everyone seeing the pictures..."

Spence opened the door. "Then let's ease in slowly."

Inside, the rest of the group had already arrived—Megs, Katie, and Missy were perched across the beds in full hot tub attire, chatting and laughing in their swimsuits. Of course Megs matched perfectly, floral print and all, looking like a poster for island glam.

"Hey, you made it!" Megs jumped up to open the door wider. "We've been waiting! Did you bring the photos?"

Grace took a deep breath. "Yep. Right here."

Katie grinned from the bed. "Missy's been hyping up the whole tour. I can't wait to see what you captured."

Missy nodded eagerly. "Seriously. The stuff Tameron said? Wild. If you got even half of that in photos, I want copies."

Grace tried to respond, but the words caught in her throat. She rubbed her palms against her pants as she set the package on the desk.

"So, no McKay yet?" Spence asked, glancing around.

"He's probably doing wardrobe changes," Spence joked. "Or choosing which of his seventeen swimsuits goes best with his towel."

Everyone laughed.

"You've never met anyone like my cousin," Spence said. "McKay is a force. I'll give him that."

Right on cue, a knock sounded at the door.

Megs opened it with a flourish. "Speak of the peacock!"

McKay strolled in, towel draped around his neck and a grin on his face. "Hope I didn't miss anything!"

Spence took the bag of clothes McKay handed over. "Mind if I borrow your bathroom?"

"Go for it," Megs said. "But hurry! We're dying to see the photos."

While Spence disappeared, Grace dug through her suitcase for her backup swimsuit. She had no intention of putting it on just yet, but she needed to do something with her hands.

The nervousness returned in full force. She'd spent more money on developing film than she planned. And she hadn't even looked at the prints yet. What if they were all blurry? What if the lighting was bad? What if she'd missed every shot she'd imagined?

Her fingers brushed over the envelopes and CDs.

"Did you start showing off the pictures yet?" McKay asked.

"Nope. They got here, too," Katie said.

As if on cue, Spence stepped out of the bathroom. He wore long swim trunks and a simple VCU t-shirt—but somehow, Grace's heart forgot how to beat normally.

She shoved a packet of prints at Missy.

Then Katie.

Then Megs. Then McKay.

She handed one to Spence, their fingers brushing for just a second.

And then she sat heavily on the bed, two envelopes still in her lap, her stomach doing somersaults.

She opened the first. The photo on top nearly made her gasp. The Temple at Chichen Itza—framed perfectly, bathed in the richest sky-blue she'd ever seen. The light. The color. The scale.

It was... breathtaking.

She flipped through more, each one a little miracle. The exposure had held. The framing was solid. The focus crisp. Even the spontaneous shots—candids of the group laughing, dramatic ruins, close-ups of carvings—turned out better than she dared hope.

Someone tapped her shoulder.

"Oh—sorry," Grace said, startled.

"These pictures rock." Missy held up a print from earlier that day—a candid of Missy and Spence standing in front of a temple, framed by a palm tree and afternoon light.

Grace barely registered the compliment before Katie chimed in.

"Oh my gosh... that's it!" Grace reached for the print Katie now held up. "That's the shot I was hoping for!"

Katie looked surprised. "Really?"

Grace's voice was breathless. "This morning I had this scrapbook layout in my head, but I needed one perfect photo for the center. I knew what I wanted, but I didn't think I'd actually get it..."

Everyone gathered to look.

They passed the print from hand to hand, oohing and ahhing like it was a rare jewel.

"Grace, you are something else," Missy said. "This is gorgeous."

"It looks like a postcard," Megs added.

"How did you do that?" McKay asked.

Grace shrugged, eyes misty. "I just... point and shoot."

"You're being far too modest," Missy said, wagging her finger at her.

Spence didn't say anything right away. But when she looked over, he wasn't flipping through his own prints.

He was watching her.

And smiling.

Grace looked down at the picture in her hands. Somehow, this cruise had become something so much bigger than she expected.

And this?

This moment might be her favorite frame yet.

Chapter 53

Spence completely agreed with Missy's assessment: Grace was being far too modest. The photos spread before them didn't just look good—they looked like they belonged in a gallery. Or a travel magazine. Or one of those glossy coffee table books that make you dream of places you've never been.

Each image pulled him in like a memory he hadn't lived. It reminded him of flipping through National Geographic as a kid—back when he believed adventures waited just beyond the next page.

He held up a photo of the fortress from earlier that day. The sharp stone edges glowed in golden light, framed by the endless blue of sky and sea. "This one," he said. "I love this one. It makes me feel like I'm there. How did you get the colors so bright?"

Grace blushed. "I don't know, I just... uh... did?"

Spence raised an eyebrow. Her voice turned her answer into a question. "No seriously, look at these pictures. They're stunning. You have to know you're an amazing photographer."

He emphasized the word—amazing—not just for the compliment, but for the private meaning it carried. Their little joke. It surprised him how good it felt to share something like that again... something real.

Before Grace could answer, Missy chimed in, holding up a print Grace must've snapped at the beach that morning. "Look at this one! It's like something from an ad. They're walking hand-in-hand, and the lighting? It's so romantic."

"Oh yeah!" Megs bounced over. "This is totally a jewelry commercial. You can see the next frame—he's proposing, and there's this insane sparkly diamond."

"Or a travel poster," Katie added. "'Visit Scenic Tulum!' I'd go. No question."

Grace's voice was barely above a whisper. "Really? You guys see all of that in these?"

Spence watched her face—this strange blend of hope and disbelief—and realized she didn't see it. Not really. She didn't understand just how good she was.

"Yes, Grace," he said softly. "We do. You've got something special. And to think—you led me to believe you just... messed around with a camera."

"That's all I do."

Spence shook his head. "Grace, I mess around with a camera. These?" He gestured to the array of prints. "These are something else. If I lived to be 135, I'd never get anything this good. You have a gift."

It wasn't just a compliment—it was truth. The kind that felt right to say.

"Grace, honey..." Megs had gone still. For once, her voice carried no fizz, no exclamation points. "These really are amazing. I'd love some prints for my album. Maybe even frame one."

Grace blinked. "Really?"

So much emotion packed into that one word: disbelief, wonder, a quiet plea to believe it might be true.

"Really," Megs said, moving to sit beside her. "You have something none of us do."

Missy knelt in front of Grace, placing her hands on Grace's knees. "We thought we were coming to see snapshots. But these... Grace, these are art."

Katie leaned over, touching Grace's shoulder. "You don't just take pictures. You see things—frame them in a way no one else does. Spence was right."

Spence felt McKay glance at him. Neither of them spoke, not wanting to break the spell.

Finally, Grace looked up, eyes a little glassy. "Thank you. You all... you have no idea what that means to me."

The room burst into motion after that. Everyone sorted prints by favorites, passing photos back and forth, making mental lists of what they wanted copies of. Laughter and admiration bubbled freely.

Grace stepped closer to Spence, holding one last envelope.

"I don't know how to thank you," she said. "If you hadn't talked me into getting these developed... I was going to wait until I got home. Like always. I never show people my pictures until I've already scrapbooked them."

Spence smiled. "Then I'm really glad I pushed. Because this—" he waved toward the happy chaos— "this is what you deserve."

Before he could stop himself, he pulled her into a hug.

And she hugged him right back.

No awkwardness. No hesitation.

Just warmth.

And for the first time in a long while, it didn't feel weird or risky.

It felt... natural.

Spence didn't let go right away. Neither did Grace.

And for that one perfect moment, all the noise in his head —memories, fears, doubts—went still.

Chapter 54

"So then, you'll never believe what Spence did next..." McKay leaned back against the curved wall of the hot tub like he was spinning the climax of a grand tale. Grace was pretty sure Spence's current desire was to launch his cousin across the deck.

Missy splashed a little water in Spence's direction. "Come on, what? You gonna tell us, or do we need McKay to do the honors?"

Spence reached for his cup at the edge of the hot tub, flicked the umbrella into a nearby trash bin, and took a sip. "I'm not the one spinning this saga. And McKay? About to win the gold medal in exaggeration."

"Whatever, cuz—you *know* it happened just like this."

"Not the way I remember it."

"Maybe not the way you *want* to remember it," McKay shot back with a grin.

"Hey now," Megs splashed both guys lightly, "just tell us already! We're dying here!"

"Fine, fine." McKay relented. "So there's Spence—standing in the bedroom of the hottest girl in the tri-ward area. In one hand? A bag of candy. In the other? A laundry basket that had held some of the clothes he just threw all over her room."

Spence groaned. "It was *one* basket of laundry. A small one! That her mom gave me!"

"But what does he do when she walks in and sees the mess? He panics—holds out the candy and says, 'Uh... my friend paid me to do this?' He says he was there to ask her to Homecoming for someone else!" McKay added triumphantly.

"Wait." Katie blinked. "Why didn't you just ask her yourself?"

"Are you *kidding* me?" Spence looked horrified at the memory. "She was *furious*. I thought she was going to jump on my back and beat me senseless. I was doing anything I could to dodge her wrath."

"Aha! I *told* you that's how it happened!" McKay pointed at Spence with the glee of a sibling who just won Christmas.

"Spence, that's amazing," Missy said with mock solemnity. "So... did she at least appreciate the candy?"

"She told me to get better friends and shoved me out the door."

Megs gasped, holding her hands to her heart. "But... you did go to Homecoming, right?"

"She called me a couple days later and apologized," Spence admitted. "Then asked me to go."

Katie leaned forward. "So she forgave you? And asked you out?"

"Not before she heart-attacked his locker," McKay added.

"Wait—what's that mean?" Katie looked around.

"Oh, sweetie," Megs sighed dramatically. "Total convert moment. You don't know what a heart attack is?"

"It's when someone covers your door or locker with hearts and love notes," Missy explained. "It's a whole thing."

"She went all out," McKay said. "Construction paper, doilies, glued-on candy hearts. Even a balloon taped to the locker door."

Grace laughed. "That's intense. But kind of cute."

"I'll tell you what wasn't cute," Spence muttered. "My sisters took photos and sent them to every relative we've got."

"Sounds like my brothers." Missy shook her head. "They made it their life's mission to make sure I never dated. That's what happens when you have seven of them. All older."

Spence winced. "Oof. I feel that with my sisters. You haven't lived until you've fought for a bathroom against teenage girls."

"Did you ever get them back?" Grace asked, grinning.

"I tried. I never could get them back for anything successfully. I swear something always backfired. The worst time was when I hid my sister's makeup in the garage. It melted." He sighed. "Didn't mean to ruin it. Just wanted some mirror time."

"And then?" Missy asked, clearly enjoying this.

Spence looked skyward. "A month later, Bishop calls me in for a PPI and again asks if I'm being a good example to my sisters. I swear he was obsessed with me being a good example to them. I wanted to say, 'Have you met my sisters?'"

The group burst into laughter. Grace clutched her ribs.

"Yeah," she added, "that's when you know it's bad—when you're praying the Bishop asks you to speak in sacrament meeting instead."

Chapter 55

Once the laughter died down, Missy turned to Grace with a teasing smile. "So what about you? Any epic sibling stories?"

Grace shrugged. "Not really. I only have one brother, and he's way older—like a decade ahead of me. We didn't have the kind of drama you guys did growing up."

Megs leaned forward conspiratorially. "No chaotic sibling rivalries? What did you get into, then?"

Grace gave a small laugh, knowing exactly what story she'd have to tell. "Okay, well... I don't have a sibling story, but I do have a prom story that's almost as bad."

She cleared her throat. "So my best friend had a crush on this guy in Chess Club—super nerdy, super quiet—but really sweet. She wanted to ask him to prom, but wanted it to be, you know, memorable. Her words."

Spence grinned. "This is already going somewhere good."

"Well, apparently he was a creature of habit. Same route home every day. Always left the back door unlocked. Always. So... we decided to sneak into his house and set up a chessboard with the king and queen in the middle, with a note that said: 'I want to be your queen. Will you go to prom with me?'"

Katie gasped. "Wait—what?"

Missy's eyes widened. "You broke into his house?"

Grace held up her hands. "Technically, the door was open. But yes... we snuck in. And just as we were leaving, his dad came home."

Megs clutched her chest. "Noooo."

"He was the town sheriff."

The entire group groaned and laughed at once.

McKay shook his head. "You did not get hauled in by the police over a prom proposal."

"Oh, we absolutely got taken to the station. I guess because it was technically trespassing and truancy."

Katie covered her mouth. "Did your parents kill you?"

"Almost. My mom was mortified. My dad just kept shaking his head like I'd personally disgraced the family name."

Spence, barely holding back laughter, asked, "Did you at least get out of trouble?"

"Actually, yes. His son—the guy my friend liked—loved the gesture. Said it was the coolest thing anyone had ever done for him. He told his dad he'd basically invited it by bragging about his unlocked door."

Spence leaned in with mock seriousness. "Okay, but the real question: did they go to prom?"

Grace nodded. "They did. And they dated for like... three months, which is practically marriage in high school terms."

"Wow." McKay shook his head. "I'm not sure what amazes me more—that you pulled it off or that the sheriff didn't book you just to teach you a lesson."

Grace grinned. "Oh, he definitely wanted to. But once his kid started calling us legends, he backed down."

Missy laughed so hard she had to wipe her eyes. "That's incredible. Best prom story I've ever heard."

Megs chimed in, "Seriously. And here I thought I was being brave asking my seminary crush out with a plate of cookies."

"Cookies are safe," Grace said with mock solemnity. "Cookies don't get you detained."

Spence chuckled, then gave her a long, quiet look. There was something about the way Grace told stories—equal parts chaos and heart. She didn't try to impress anyone. She just was. And Spence found that incredibly refreshing.

As the group quieted again, the hot tub's gentle bubbles filled the silence.

Grace leaned her arms on the edge and looked up at the stars. "You know, I never expected this trip to be so fun."

Missy nodded. "Me either. I mean, I knew it'd be something, but I didn't think I'd be sitting in a hot tub with a bunch of people I only met a few days ago and feeling like I've known them for years."

Megs raised her drink. "To unexpected friendships."

"Here, here," McKay echoed, clinking his glass with hers.

Spence lifted his own cup and nudged Grace's arm. "To second chances."

Grace smiled, soft and sincere, and tapped her cup to his. "Second chances."

And under the stars, surrounded by the laughter of new friends and the quiet hum of connection, Grace felt something shift inside her—a warmth that had nothing to do with the hot tub.

She wasn't just surviving anymore.

She was beginning to live again.

Chapter 56

Grace quietly gathered the stacks of photographs while Megs sang in the shower. The noise gave her cover—a little privacy to breathe and sit with the whirlwind of emotions still buzzing beneath her skin.

She sifted through the prints with gentler fingers now, as if she might better understand herself if she could just see her life reflected through the lens. Her friends and family had always said she had an eye for composition. She never quite believed them. But tonight... tonight had been different.

Their praise had felt real.

Earnest.

Overwhelming.

How strange, that these veritable strangers had seen her more clearly than people who'd known her for years. She picked up one of the group's favorite shots—the sun setting just behind a crumbling temple wall, the light catching in all the right places—and held it up, turning it in her hand like a treasure. Maybe... just maybe... it would look good in an 8x10 with a mat. She had a bare spot on her bedroom wall that had been crying out for something meaningful.

She was still admiring the photo when Megs' voice floated in from the bathroom.

"So... what do you think of McKay?"

Grace blinked, caught off guard. "What?"

"Well, you and he seemed to hit it off at first. But now he and Missy are spending more time together. I just wondered... was something going on there? With you and him?"

Grace turned toward the bathroom door, trying to bite back the sharpness in her tone. "What do you mean?"

"I mean, you and McKay were always hanging out at the beginning, and now... I don't know. Maybe it looked like there was something more? But you don't act like it. So... is there?"

Grace forced herself to breathe. "We're friends. That's all."

Megs hesitated, then said carefully, "I didn't mean anything bad. I just thought maybe something could happen. I mean, sometimes things do, even when you're not looking for it."

Grace's jaw tightened. "Well, I'm not looking. I told you from the beginning—I'm not here to find someone. I'm here to relax. Recharge. Be a person again, not just a mom."

She paused, the words catching in her throat. "Besides... even if I was open to something, I haven't met anyone who lives anywhere near me. I have a child to think about."

The bathroom fell quiet for a moment, the water still running in the background.

Grace sighed. "I just wish..."

She didn't finish the sentence. What did she wish?

To be more like Megs—bubbly, open, full of hope and excitement about love again? Maybe. Once upon a time, maybe she had been that girl. She couldn't even remember anymore.

Megs' voice was soft when she finally responded. "I just thought... I mean, Spence is really nice. And the two of you seem to click."

Grace didn't answer at first. Her mind had already started spiraling down that all-too-familiar path. Missy and Spence. That would make more sense, wouldn't it? They had things in common. Mission stories. Shared faith backgrounds. A sibling connection. A spark that didn't feel forced.

And if they did get together?

Where would that leave her?

Friendless. Again.

Because once people paired off, there was no space for single friends. Not in social plans. Not in spiritual settings. Not in life.

She pressed her palm flat against the photograph in her lap. The picture didn't change. It was still beautiful. But something inside her dimmed.

Ridiculous, she scolded herself. She'd known Spence for what—three days? She didn't have a claim on him. Not even close. Still, the pang in her chest was real. Sharp, even.

She didn't want to think anymore.

She just wanted to sleep.

Grace tucked the last of the photographs into her suitcase and zipped it shut with a sigh. Megs was still humming away in the bathroom.

Without another word, Grace crawled into bed and pulled the blankets up to her chin.

"Going to bed already?" Megs called out.

Grace stared at the ceiling. "Yeah. I'm just... tired."

It wasn't a lie.

But it wasn't the whole truth either.

Chapter 57

With McKay finally done monopolizing the tiny cruise cabin bathroom, Spence grabbed his shaving kit and stepped in, the mirror already fogged with steam. He lathered his face and began to shave slowly, thoughtfully—his mind spinning more than his razor.

He felt something for Grace. There was no denying it anymore. He wasn't about to declare his undying love or anything—he wasn't ready for that. But the fear he used to feel about getting close? That was gone.

Whatever this was between them, it mattered.

Maybe it was just friendship. Maybe it would be more.

And for the first time in a long time, maybe more didn't terrify him.

He groaned quietly, shaking his head at his reflection. He was so rusty at this. This being... whatever this was. Dating? Feelings? He'd never been particularly skilled at romance to begin with. In high school, his social life consisted of major dances and youth group events—carefully overseen by his parents and his ever-watchful sisters.

Sometimes being the only boy had its downsides.

But it had paid off. At nineteen, he left with no attachments, ready to serve. Two years on a mission changed him in ways he never expected. And when he returned, he was ready. Ready for love, ready for marriage.

Ready for Julie.

Their relationship had moved quickly, even by Latter-day Saint standards. And yet, despite all the caution, all the prayer, it hadn't worked out. The marriage had unraveled.

For so long, that failure lived in his chest like a fist. But tonight? Tonight he could think about Julie without that same ache. The bitterness had dulled. Maybe, just maybe, he was ready to believe again—in love, in possibilities, in himself.

He wiped the fog from the mirror and stared at his face for a long moment. Older. Maybe a little wiser. Definitely more tired. But maybe, too, a little more whole than he'd been in years.

Showered and wrapped in a towel, he cracked open the bathroom door to let the steam out—and nearly jumped out of his skin.

"What on earth are you wearing?" he asked, gaping at McKay.

"This?" McKay turned in place like a model on a runway. "This is my Pimpzilla hat. Thinking I might wear it tomorrow to impress the ladies."

The hat was an unholy fusion of neon purple, green, and orange, with a stuffed Godzilla-like creature perched on top like a throne.

"You'll impress someone," Spence said, sipping his drink and squinting at the monstrosity.

"I'm thinking Uncle Blaine would love this."

Spence burst out laughing. "Oh man. That's... actually perfect."

Uncle Blaine, the family fashion disaster. Colorblind. Possibly taste-blind. He wasn't much older than Spence, but you'd never know it. His wardrobe consisted of pants that hit his chest, mismatched patterns, and shirts that made your eyes water.

"Can you see him in this hat?" McKay beamed.

"Oh, I can see it. Pair it with that mint green and Pepto-Bismol pink plaid shirt? Instant fashion apocalypse."

"Don't forget the 1970s tie with the giant orange flowers."

Spence groaned. "Nightmare fuel."

"You started it."

"You brought it into this cabin."

"I regret nothing."

Spence eyed the Godzilla. "Is the lizard eating the flower on top?"

"I think so. The real question is—will he eat the hat next?"

"If there's any mercy in the universe, yes."

McKay held it up thoughtfully. "Still... maybe I'll give it to Uncle Blaine. Or save it for Halloween. It has youth activity written all over it."

"Just make sure I'm there to see the look on his face."

As Spence moved to get dressed, he rummaged through his neatly organized drawer and pulled out his sleep clothes. That's when McKay's tone shifted, a little more serious.

"So... what do you think about Missy?"

Spence paused. "Missy?"

"I think she might like you."

Spence blinked. "No way."

"I'm serious. You've got two girls paying you attention, man. You might end up with something happening on this cruise even if you weren't looking for it. I'm jealous."

"You? Jealous? You and Megs were practically joined at the hip on the beach."

McKay shrugged with a grin. "Megs is great. We ran into each other and just started talking. She's fun. Can you believe she tried to talk me into snorkeling?"

"Snorkeling, huh?"

"Yeah. We almost did it, but the place was closing."

"Maybe we could try it tomorrow?" McKay suggested.

Spence hesitated. He wanted to say yes, but... Tikal. That site had been on his bucket list forever. Besides, there was Grace. He wanted to know what she planned to do.

"I don't know. I'll have to see."

"Aw, come on! Once in a lifetime! 'I went snorkeling off the coast of South America' sounds way cooler than 'I waded into the Atlantic at Myrtle Beach.'"

"True... but Tikal."

"You're killing me, man. What is Tikal, anyway?"

Spence smirked. "Just for that, I'll let you dwindle in unbelief."

McKay chucked a pillow at him, and Spence tossed it right back, laughter bouncing off the cabin walls.

Chapter 58

Spence eyed the group strapped into mismatched safety harnesses and shook his head. Had he really sacrificed time at Tikal for a zip line tour? He could practically hear the guidebooks scolding him. But when he saw Grace's anxious face earlier that morning, something tugged inside him—something that told him this was worth more than ancient stone temples.

She needed this.

He could tell Grace was used to putting herself last. Used to missing out, talking herself out of adventure. But not today. Not if he could help it.

And maybe... he needed it too.

He thought of Megs chattering about a guy she dated who took her zip-lining, and suddenly he remembered a younger version of himself—the one who went hiking, biking, rock climbing. Who lived life without holding back.

Where had that guy gone?

"You sure this is safe?" Grace asked—for what had to be the tenth time in ten minutes.

"YES!" came the unified groan from the group.

Even Katie, who looked pale and ready to bolt, mustered a thumbs-up.

"OK, OK," Grace muttered. "I just... that platform is moving, right?"

"It might be," McKay said with a shrug. "Think of it like a suspension bridge."

Grace looked horrified. "I hate bridges!"

McKay grinned. "Good! Then this'll help you get over it."

"Not helping," she whispered.

Missy gave her a quick side-hug. "Don't worry. They clip you in before you even step off the ladder. Total safety. I promise."

"Couldn't they just... put up a real safety net?"

"That'd be a lot of net," McKay pointed out. "We're in a rainforest, not Cirque du Soleil."

"Still..."

Grace's protests trailed off as the zip-line operator called out: "Who's up?"

McKay stepped forward. "That's me."

The staff clipped him into a belay rope and checked his harness. Spence watched McKay climb, noting how Grace's eyes never left him. She was locked in, watching every carabiner, every step.

When McKay reached the top, he waved, then zipped off the platform with a triumphant "WHEEEEEEEE!"

Katie gulped. "Guess that's the cue."

Before Grace could redirect the spotlight, Katie stepped forward. "I better go now before I chicken out."

Grace bit her lip. "Maybe I should—"

"Nope! You're next," Missy cut her off. "We're not letting you chicken out. Spence and I have both done this before. You've got this."

Grace sighed. "Fine..."

From above came a sudden high-pitched scream. The group craned their necks to see Katie flying down the line, feet flailing and laughter trailing in her wake.

"You're up!"

Grace's legs moved before her brain agreed. The staff clipped her into the belay rope and gestured toward the ladder. "All set. Just climb, and they'll handle the rest at the top."

"Relax," he added. "The view's worth it."

Grace wasn't convinced. But she climbed anyway.

Each rung felt like a small mountain. Halfway up, her arms ached. Her breath came in short bursts, and she stopped for a moment, head tilted toward the canopy. She could do this. She had to do this.

When she reached the top, a man extended his hand. "Welcome to the sky."

She managed a weak smile.

"It's scarier here than on the line, I promise. Just stay relaxed, and I'll talk you through everything."

Grace nodded, not trusting her voice.

"We're switching your clips now, one at a time. You're still fully secured. I'll let you know when you're officially on the zip line."

She watched him work. Her heart pounded, but the calm in his voice helped.

"Okay, all set. Now—how do you want to do this? You can step off. You can run. Or... I can give you a little help."

"Uh—"

"Help it is!"

Before she could panic again, he gave a gentle shove—and she was flying.

Chapter 59

Grace screamed—but not in fear.

The zip line caught her mid-air, sending her soaring across the canopy in a flash of wind and exhilaration. Leaves blurred past in vibrant greens. The sky above was impossibly blue. Below her stretched an endless sea of rainforest, wild and unbroken. And for the first time in what felt like forever, she wasn't thinking.

Not about work.

Not about bills.

Not about Aaron's next growth spurt or the stain on the carpet she couldn't afford to fix.

She was just flying.

By the time she reached the end platform, her heart was racing, her cheeks were flushed, and she was laughing. The sound surprised even her.

"Drop the rope!" someone below called.

She glanced down at the safety line still slung over her shoulder and tossed it to the ground with a grin. Two ladders clattered into place, and an operator climbed up with the kind of ease that made Grace think he'd been born part monkey.

"Wasn't it fun?" McKay shouted as she descended.

"Holy wowee cow!" Grace shouted back.

The phrase tumbled out before she could stop it. She barely hit the ground before she clapped a hand over her mouth, eyes wide.

McKay blinked. "Holy... what now?"

"I... I don't know! It just popped out!"

McKay grinned. "I'm keeping it. That's my new catchphrase. Holy wowee cow. It's gold."

Grace laughed harder. "Great. Make sure I get royalties when it ends up on a T-shirt at BYU."

"Oh, I will. It'll be bigger than funeral potatoes at ward potlucks."

The group was still laughing when Grace noticed Katie, silent and still at the edge of the clearing. Her face had gone pale, her arms folded tightly across her chest.

Grace's laughter faded, replaced with concern.

"Katie? You alright?"

Katie hesitated, then nodded, but it was the kind of nod that didn't reach her eyes.

"That was just... the craziest thing I've ever done," she admitted softly. "I don't think I've caught my breath yet."

Grace stepped closer. "You're not hurt, are you?"

"No. Not... not physically." Katie gave a shaky smile. "It's like my body's down here, but my brain's still ziplining over the rainforest."

Grace gently placed a hand on her shoulder. "That was me five minutes ago. I was sure I was going to pass out or throw up—or both. But look." She motioned to the group. "We're all here. And we're okay."

Katie's shoulders relaxed the smallest bit. "You looked like you had fun."

"I did." Grace surprised herself with the honesty of it. "Once the terror passed, it was kind of... freeing. Like I'd finally outrun all the stuff in my head."

Katie nodded slowly, her expression softening. "That makes sense. I guess I wasn't expecting so much emotion. I just thought it'd be a thrill."

"Turns out, sometimes thrills bring the baggage with them," Grace said gently. "Come sit for a minute."

She steered Katie toward a fallen log just off the trail where the trees cast a cool shade. The other girls followed without hesitation, surrounding Katie with quiet encouragement.

Spence lingered back, watching Grace carefully. Her hair was wind-tousled, her cheeks still flushed, her eyes lit with adrenaline. She looked alive in a way he hadn't seen before. Not just happy. Empowered.

And seeing her comfort Katie like that? Yeah... she had that quiet kind of strength. The kind that didn't demand attention—but earned it.

Missy leaned closer to Spence and nudged his elbow. "She was brave, huh?"

He didn't answer right away.

"Yeah," he said finally. "She really was."

They all rested there a while, sipping from their water bottles and sharing their reactions to the ride. Megs raved about the view. McKay compared the sensation to riding Space Mountain in the dark. Katie eventually cracked a real smile, and Grace leaned back against the log, feeling the ground beneath her feet like a promise.

When it was time to go, Spence walked beside her on the trail.

"You know," he said, nudging her lightly with his shoulder, "you made that look way too easy."

Grace snorted. "Easy? Did you not see me almost faint climbing the ladder?"

"Sure, but once you were airborne? You had the biggest smile I've seen all trip."

She glanced sideways at him. "I think I needed that."

"Yeah. Me too."

They shared a smile and walked on in companionable silence.

Ahead, McKay was loudly reenacting his jungle battle cry, and the girls were teasing him mercilessly. Grace chuckled and shook her head. Spence just grinned.

The rainforest thinned, and the trail turned toward the vans that would take them back to the ship. Grace took one last look back at the canopy.

She'd flown through that.

And tomorrow?

She wasn't planning to come back down.

Chapter 60

"So what's going on over there?" Spence unhooked his harness, squinting in the sunlight as he motioned toward the small huddle of Grace and Katie.

"Katie's just a little freaked out," McKay replied, collecting harnesses with all the nonchalance of a summer camp counselor. "I don't think this was her deal."

"Yeah. It's not for everyone." Spence nodded, glancing again toward Grace. "What about her? Grace do okay?"

McKay grinned. "Oh my heck. You'll never guess what she said! When I asked her how it was? She goes, 'Holy wowee cow.' Can you believe that? Isn't that the most Utah thing you've ever heard?"

Spence tilted his head, trying the phrase out in his mind. "Holy wowee cow," he echoed. "Yeah. That's... actually kind of great."

McKay laughed. "Right? I'm totally stealing it."

"Too late," Spence said with a grin, "I was just thinking the same thing."

"Hey, here—give me your harness. I'll take it over with the others."

Spence handed over the gear and gave a long, lazy stretch, reaching his arms overhead until his back popped. That felt good. Flying over the rainforest had been... unexpected. Thrilling. Alive. He turned to make his way toward Grace and Katie when his foot caught a slope in the uneven earth.

His ankle rolled sideways just as Missy stepped off the ladder in front of him—and the two collided in a clumsy heap.

"What on earth—?" Missy landed with a yelp, pinned beneath Spence's limbs and an unfortunate tangle of straps.

"I'm really sorry!" Spence scrambled to untangle himself, only managing to shift in the same direction as Missy. They ended up bumping into each other all over again. "I don't know what happened. I just lost my balance."

He finally managed to stand and offered his hand to help her up. Missy looked like she wasn't sure whether to laugh or groan as she dusted herself off.

"It's alright. That was just… a mess." She flicked a stray leaf from her shoulder, still not quite looking at him.

Spence winced. That hadn't helped anything. The day had been going so well, and now he felt like he'd just turned it into an awkward tangle of limbs and misunderstandings. Smooth, Olsen. Real smooth.

"I really am sorry," he offered again, testing his ankle with a cautious wiggle. A little sore, but not terrible.

Missy was preoccupied with her harness. "It's okay. Accidents happen. I just can't seem to get this one clip undone."

Spence hesitated. The clip in question sat near her waist—awkward territory. "Want help? If you're okay with that."

"Would you mind? It's really stuck."

"Sure." He stepped in, careful and professional, fingers working at the finicky clip. The harness was all loops and buckles and crossed straps—who designed these things anyway? Finally, the mechanism gave with a snap and began to loosen.

They both reached to catch the gear at the same time, and their hands brushed—just for a second. Spence stepped back quickly to give her space, pretending not to notice the momentary awkwardness.

"Thanks," Missy said, gathering the rest of the gear. "That thing was really stubborn."

"No kidding." He gestured toward the group. "I'm gonna go sit down while you take those over?"

"Sure thing."

As Spence turned toward the rest of the group, he caught them all staring at him.

"What was that about?" McKay asked the question casually, but there was a mischievous glint in his eye.

Spence flopped to the ground beside the group, rotating his sore ankle gently. "That was me being stupid. I turned my ankle."

McKay raised a brow. "Stupid? I dunno. Looked like a well-timed meet-cute."

Spence groaned. "Don't start."

"Too late. I've seen that scene in a dozen rom-coms."

Spence shook his head, focusing on his foot. It wasn't swollen, thankfully. He pointed and flexed, rolled it left, then right. Tender, but manageable. Definitely not enough to keep him from climbing Tikal tomorrow.

He glanced up to see Missy sitting a little ways off now, quietly rejoining the group. She didn't look upset. Still, he didn't like how awkward that had gotten.

"Dude." McKay leaned over. "You okay?"

"Yeah." Spence nodded. "I just didn't want to step wrong, that's all."

"You sure? You looked like you took a tumble worthy of high school gym class."

Spence offered a thin smile. "Pretty sure I've had worse doing stake dance choreography."

McKay burst out laughing. "Touché."

As they sat and waited for the rest of the group to return, Spence stretched his ankle out in front of him and tilted his head back to take in the view of the canopy above. The jungle really was beautiful. Alive. And he felt... clearer.

Grace was laughing softly now with Katie, who looked a lot less pale than before. The two of them were deep in conversation, but Grace looked up and caught Spence's eye. Just for a second. She smiled—small, sincere, a little shy—and he smiled back.

And somehow, in that split second, the awkward tumble, the twisted ankle, the nerves... all of it felt worth it.

Chapter 61

Grace couldn't stop replaying the image of Spence falling into Missy. The tangle of limbs. The awkward attempt to untangle. The lingering moment that might've meant nothing... or something.

She sighed—a sound more frustrated than she meant it to be.

"Is everything OK?" Spence's voice came from just to her left, but she barely acknowledged him.

"Nothing." It came out flat, mumbled more to herself than him.

Ahead of them, Katie, McKay, and Megs strolled along, animated in conversation. Grace tuned her ears toward them, hoping distraction would tame the thoughts chasing each other through her head.

"So then I told my companion..." McKay's storytelling was already in full swing. Something about his mission in Chile. Grace smirked. Of course. Megs would eat that up.

"A machete? No!" Megs slapped a hand to her mouth, eyes wide with delight. "Really?"

"Yeah, he chased us across a field screaming in Spanish. Something about us heathens rotting in hell for eternity."

"All because you talked about Joseph Smith?" Katie gasped.

"Either that, or he just didn't like prophets," McKay replied. "Either way, he wasn't too subtle."

Grace had no idea how the story started, but the mental image made her snort. She imagined two well-dressed missionaries sprinting through fields like a religious buddy comedy.

The sound made the three in front stop and turn.

Grace nearly walked into Megs.

"What was that?" McKay grinned and winked at her.

"Sorry," she laughed, lifting a hand. "I was just picturing the missionaries from back home doing that. You running in a suit and tie from a machete-wielding farmer? That's a visual."

Her laughter surprised even her. For a moment, the annoyance about Spence and Missy evaporated.

They started walking again as a group, headed for the temples of Tikal. Grace decided the more the merrier. Or, at least, the better to let Spence and Missy pal around without her getting in the way.

That's it, she told herself. They just clicked. Some people do. She'd seen it at church a hundred times—instant connections that led to whirlwind engagements. Why should this be any different?

She hated how much that thought stung.

She drifted further into the group, letting McKay's stories distract her.

"How far are we from Chile?" Missy asked, glancing back at McKay.

"Well, we're still in Central America," McKay replied. "Which is technically part of North America. Chile's way down on the west coast of South America—about two-thirds of the way down."

Katie blinked. "I always thought Chile was more west than us."

"We're actually pretty far east here," Grace chimed in. "Think like... Florida or Alabama. Chile's on the west coast, but it's really only south from where we are. A lot of South America is actually further east than the USA."

"That's weird."

"Southern Hemisphere will do that to you," McKay added. "Makes everything feel upside down. It's better to think of Chili as being in the Eastern Time Zone. Sometimes they are!"

He slung an arm around each girl. "It's wild writing home in July and saying, 'It's snowing!' and getting a letter back that's like, 'It's 110 degrees, send help.'"

"That's so strange." Missy shook her head. "And I hate daylight savings time. I thought it was just us in the States!"

"Oh no, they've got it, too," McKay said. "And it's backwards from ours. Which really messes with you when you're trying to call home."

Spence turned toward the group as Megs asked, "What about Perth?"

"Perth rocks," he said with a wistful smile. "It's this tropical, coastal dream. Water so clear you can see to the bottom."

"But you couldn't swim, right?"

"Nope. Mission rules. And I missed it. Every day."

"You were a swimmer?" Missy asked.

"Big time," McKay jumped in. "He was nearly Olympic-bound."

That did it. The focus shifted straight back to McKay, and Megs fawned accordingly.

Grace barely heard the rest. Her thoughts had drifted again—this time to Perth. She wanted to ask Spence more. What it was like. What he missed about it. If he ever wanted to go back.

But she didn't ask. Not with Missy there. Not with her mood still tangled.

Instead, she walked in silence, listening to the laughter ahead and hating how much it hurt.

Chapter 62

"What do you guys think? I think this hat makes me look like Indiana Jones." McKay struck a pose as he modeled a battered leather safari hat for the group.

"Oh absolutely," Megs said with mock reverence, eyes wide. "It's so you."

"I think so too. I'm rugged. I'm sexy. All the girls are gonna want me now."

Katie gave him a theatrical once-over. "Oh, baby. It totally makes you. I think you have to buy it."

"Me too. It's sold!" He held the hat like a trophy.

"Holy wowee cow! I just got the best idea!" Megs spun toward Grace. "Grace, you up for taking some ridiculous pictures?"

"Uh... I guess so? What kind of ridiculous are we talking about?"

"I'm talking adventure movie posters. You know? Big ruins in the background. 'Indiana Jones meets Latter-day Date Night.'"

"Uh... maybe?"

"OK, super simple. Look—McKay, get over here." Megs yanked McKay in front of a massive stone temple and shoved him into position. "Stand like you're the studmeister of all time."

McKay planted his feet wide, hands on his hips, chin high. "That's right, ladies. I am the ultimate studmeister. All other men pale before me."

"I always said you were an Old Spice guy," Spence called from behind Grace.

McKay smirked. "That's right, ladies. Sadly, your man is not the studmeister of all time. I am."

Grace tried to hold back a laugh, but her shoulders shook. "OK, so... then what?"

"Then we get some of the girls to lean on him, like he's all that and a salami sandwich." Megs motioned to Katie. "Come on, just mirror me."

Megs draped herself dramatically across McKay's left side, hands splayed on his chest, gaze fixed upward. Katie mirrored the pose on his right, fighting laughter.

"Picture it," Megs said. "A giant temple behind us. McKay doing his best fake GQ face. It's perfect. Like a parody poster for Return to the Jungle: Mormon Edition."

McKay struck a model pose. "Studmeister. Legend. Danger. Also really good at seminary."

Grace cracked, laughter bubbling out. The tension Spence had seen in her shoulders seemed to finally lift. Her eyes sparkled—and Spence couldn't stop looking at her. That spark of mischief, of joy—it was the most beautiful thing he'd seen all day. Even more than soaring across the rainforest.

"OK, I'm game," Grace said, still giggling. "Let's absolutely do it."

Megs and Katie high-fived over McKay's chest and peeled off to prep the props. McKay returned to the vendor to haggle over the fedora while Megs hunted down a long purple scarf to complete the ensemble.

Spence stood off to the side, relieved to see Grace laughing again, but still worried. Something shifted after the zip lines. She'd been... quieter. Distant. And not with everyone—just with him. She'd responded to the others, even joked around. But with him?

Nothing. Walls.

McKay insisted Grace had a blast on the zip line—so what changed? Did he do something wrong? Had he missed something?

He hated this feeling. Like there was a secret code everyone else could read but he couldn't crack. It reminded him a little too much of his marriage. The silent expectations. The confusion. The slow unraveling.

He shook the thought away. This wasn't that. This was different. He hoped it was different.

Still, it stung. And it left him wondering... How do you get a woman to forgive you for something you don't even know you did?

Grace's laughter rang out again, light and full of life. Spence looked toward the ruins towering in the distance and followed the group, determined to stick close—even if he had no idea how to fix things.

Given enough time, he thought, maybe I'll figure it out.

Chapter 63

Taking pictures proved cathartic for Grace. She actually felt glamorous—and for once, like she belonged in the middle of something joyful. People were even moving out of her way to avoid ruining the shot. That never happened. Normally, she had to crop strangers out of every other photo.

The group helped, of course. Their encouragement came with a steady stream of cheesy movie lines and mock modeling calls. It made everything feel surreal and wonderfully silly.

"Baby, the camera loves you. Love the camera. Want the camera. Need the camera!" Spence called to the pair in front of her lens.

Since they were goofing off anyway, Spence had handed her his digital camera and told her to shoot with that. The ability to preview her shots immediately was addictive. Would it be wrong to say she'd already fallen in love with his camera? Like, ready-to-run-off-into-the-sunset love? She might whisper sweet nothings to its lens later.

For someone who normally only photographed candid shots or her son in front of things, this felt like actual portraiture. And she was loving every second of it.

"Let's do one with all of you now," she said, scanning the stepped temple behind them.

"This'll be our first all-group photo! Exciting!" Katie bounced on her toes, clearly recovered from her earlier nerves.

Grace motioned everyone up. "Okay, I want you guys on this step—about ten up. Stand mostly back-to-back, but pivot just a bit so you're facing forward."

She slipped the camera strap over her head and used both hands to nudge Spence and McKay into position. She ran a few steps down, then stopped.

"Wait—shoulders apart some. Like... right. Not fully back-to-back, but offset. Yes! Perfect."

Back on the ground, she turned to the girls. "Okay, we're going for smoldering, sexy, movie-poster vamp. Like you're the glamorous danger girls beside your international super spies."

Megs and Missy nodded. Katie grinned. "Oh, I can totally do that."

Grace started with Megs. "Okay, I want you angled beside McKay, slightly down one step. Think femme fatale meets shampoo commercial."

Before Grace could finish the pose instruction, Megs threw herself against McKay's side, hands spread across his chest, chin tilted over her shoulder.

"How's this?" she asked, eyes narrowed dramatically.

"Perfect!" Grace laughed. "Just pout a little more and pivot that hip... good! Yes!"

Katie was already on the move. "Okay, my turn. What's the vibe?"

"Same position as Megs, but with Spence. Don't look at the camera—swoon into his arms."

"Got it. You gonna catch me, big boy?" she asked Spence with a wink.

"You know it."

Katie swooned, dramatically draping herself across Spence's chest as he braced her in place. Somehow, this didn't bother Grace like the Missy incident had. Maybe because this was pure play.

She paused. Or... maybe because she was the one who'd paired them. On purpose. She didn't want to assign those poses to Missy and Spence.

"Missy, how are your knees?"

"What? Um, fine... why?"

"I have an idea. You'd be kneeling—centered in front of them. Can you reach up and grab each guy by the thigh like you own them both? But look straight ahead. Full Palmer girl. Like you're daring the world to try and take them from you."

Missy laughed. "You mean: 'These two men are mine, and the rest of you can suck it'?"

"Exactly."

Missy knelt into place, nailing the pose with more attitude than Grace expected. It was almost intimidating.

"Okay..." Grace looked up. "McKay, look into the sky like a gladiator god. Yes, chin up. Hold it."

She stepped back and framed the shot. The angle was perfect—no tourists in view, the temple behind them kissing the brilliant blue sky. She checked her camera settings, then called out, "Ready? One... two... three!"

She pressed the shutter and held it for a burst. Then she zoomed for a tighter crop and took a few more.

"How'd they turn out?" McKay was already stepping out of the pose.

Grace squinted into the camera screen, shielding it with her hand. "I think... yes. Looks awesome!"

"Thank goodness. My arms were starting to cramp." Spence helped Katie up.

"No problem," Katie said. "My leg was falling asleep. But that was so worth it."

"Absolutely." McKay grinned. "Grace, you have to get these developed tonight. Party in our room?"

"Sounds good to me." Missy stretched her legs, brushing off her knees. "That was crazy fun. Any other ideas?"

"I can't think of anything else to try." Grace shook her head, beaming. "But seriously—thanks, you guys."

"Are you kidding? I felt like a model." Megs clapped. "Oh my gosh, Grace, please say we can post these online or something."

"Oh yeah, totally," Grace said. "These were just for fun. We all did them."

"Make sure you tag me!" Katie added. "I want everyone I know to see this. I haven't had this much fun since... ever."

Grace hesitated. "But what if the photos aren't as good as you think?"

Katie rolled her eyes. "Grace. Please. From what I saw yesterday, you don't take bad photos."

Grace ducked her head, smiling as she slipped Spence's camera back into its padded pouch. Her heart felt full.

"Wait!" Megs darted forward. "Grace, you need a crazy photo!"

"What? No—uh, I don't think—"

"Nope. Not fair. You've got all these hilarious shots of us, and we don't have a single one of you. It's, like, a moral injustice."

"She's right," Missy chimed in. "You let us be Charlie's Angels, and McKay be Indiana Jones. Now it's your turn."

"We may not be as good as you, but I'm sure that camera has an auto setting," Katie added. "Or we can fix it in Photoshop."

Grace laughed, caught off guard by their enthusiasm. "All right. One photo. Maybe two. But I'm not doing the leg drape."

"Oh don't worry," Megs said, gleeful. "I've got something better in mind."

Chapter 64

Grace marveled at the cruise ship's library. The library near her apartment was decent, but this? This was a dream. It spanned multiple floors, filled with nothing but books—shelves towering above and plunging below like some kind of literary cathedral. She leaned over the balcony, awestruck, and briefly considered moving in permanently.

Her mood lifted. She took a deep, steadying breath and imagined inhaling all the library's stories, like oxygen for the soul.

Plush armchairs, cozy love seats, and warm antique lamps filled the space. The interior designers had created a literary sanctuary, as comfortable as it was elegant. It was, she decided, exactly the kind of place her heart had been needing.

She made her way toward the periodicals. With only a little time to spare before her photos would be ready, she didn't want to commit to a novel. Something light—something fluffy—would do just fine.

She flipped through a few options before settling on a small stack of girly magazines. The kind full of quizzes and glittery font headlines. Brain candy. Perfect.

Grace found a secluded armchair nestled in a corner, offering just enough privacy to be alone with her thoughts. She sank into the chair and, for a moment, let herself miss home.

If she were back in her apartment, she and Aaron would be curled up on the sofa reading a story together. Afterward, he'd scamper off to bed, leaving her to do the dishes, maybe pay a bill or fold a load of laundry. Then she'd watch half an episode of something before heading to bed herself.

It was simple. Predictable. Quiet.

She liked the quiet.

Now, here she was, flipping through pages she wasn't reading, thinking about things she didn't want to admit.

What had set her off that morning? How had she gone from the exhilaration of the zip line—one of the most freeing, joy-filled moments she could remember—to this sour, tangled mood?

She knew the answer. She didn't want to know, but she did. And she hated that it was so cliché.

Jealousy.

It was ridiculous. It wasn't like she and Spence had anything going on. He was kind. Thoughtful. Maybe even a little flirty—but that didn't mean anything. It wasn't fair to feel possessive.

Still... seeing him fall into Missy had struck something in her. Not because of the fall itself. Accidents happened. But the way they looked together. The way he looked, flustered and handsome and perfectly at ease with someone like Missy.

Her heart had no business reacting the way it did.

This cruise was supposed to be a reset—a week of relaxation, of laughter, of maybe making some new friends. Not of catching a case of the "likes" like some teen girl at EFY. She rubbed her temples, trying to will the feelings away.

Why now? Why him?

She couldn't even remember when things started to shift. All she knew was that if someone had asked her who she'd want to spend time with for the rest of the trip, she wouldn't have hesitated.

It would be Spence.

And that made it all the more important to get a grip.

They weren't from the same state. They didn't live near each other. And Grace had a son to think about. A whole life to think about. Whatever issues Spence was sorting through, she didn't need to add hers to the pile.

Besides, he and Missy seemed to click so naturally. Grace could see it—the shared humor, the matching energy. It made sense.

And Missy? Missy was exactly the type of woman Grace would have been instant friends with under different circumstances. She was bright and funny and warm-hearted.

And Grace liked her.

Which made this even worse.

She hated the way jealousy twisted things, made everything sharper and more fragile than it needed to be. She told herself—firmly—that she could do better. That she would do better.

There were still a few days left on the cruise. She could stay polite. She could enjoy the group. She could keep her distance from Spence and focus on herself. On Aaron. On whatever quiet peace she could find.

Once the ship docked, she'd go home. He'd go home. Maybe he and Missy would fall in love and get married and have twelve kids. She'd never know.

It wasn't like they lived in the same stake. They wouldn't bump into each other at the store. Or mutual. Or Stake Conference.

She could let go.

She could. She would.

But somehow, it still made her sad.

Chapter 65

"So what on earth was up with Grace today?" McKay dabbed shaving cream onto his face in the bathroom, the door wide open.

Spence sat in the room flipping through cruise brochures, not really paying attention. "What's that?"

McKay leaned into view, half his face covered in foam. "Grace. Wasn't she acting a little weird?"

"You noticed that?"

"Uh, yeah. Hard not to. It was like... I don't know, like she was on another planet. You two seemed pretty chummy, so I figured maybe you'd know. Did she actually enjoy the zip line, or was that an act?"

Spence set the brochures aside and cracked his knuckles. "Honestly? I'm not sure. She was really nervous before going up. But after? I went over to talk to her and she just... well... she kind of gave me..."

"The cold shoulder?" McKay rinsed his razor in the sink. "Yeah, I saw that. She loosened up again for the photos, though. Thought maybe it was just a zip line thing."

"That's what I thought too. But then she clammed up again during the tour. She was totally engaged on the earlier ones. I actually thought maybe..."

He trailed off. Did he really want to admit it? Out loud?

McKay poked his head out again, hair a chaotic mess. "What? What'd you think?"

Spence sighed. "I thought maybe she was into all of it. Like me. The history, the connection to the Book of Mormon. She just... she was really excited. Not like a passing 'this is neat' thing—genuinely interested. And that's rare. It felt good."

McKay grinned. "Ha! I knew it." He emerged from the bathroom in nothing but a towel, half-shaved and still wet.

Spence would've laughed if he hadn't been feeling so off. "Yeah, well, it's not just that. It's been a long time since I met someone I could really talk to about that stuff. And not just 'talk to'—actually connect with. It's been a while."

"'Interested interested,' huh?"

"Don't start."

"I get it. You don't have to marry the girl. But you're allowed to enjoy someone's company." McKay clapped a hand on Spence's shoulder, all jokes aside for once. "It's OK."

Spence groaned and shoved him away. "Not when you're half naked and foamy. Go finish shaving."

McKay grinned and disappeared back into the bathroom.

Spence lay back on the bed and stared at the ceiling. He didn't want to fall back into the same emotional rut he'd just clawed out of, but something had shifted. Grace made him feel like life was moving again. That maybe he wasn't broken.

Not that he was about to do something idiotic like propose to someone he'd known for three days. But the fact that he wasn't terrified by the idea? That was something.

He liked Grace. He really did. And more than that, he respected her.

Maybe it wouldn't lead to anything. Maybe it would. But he wasn't ready to let this connection go when the ship docked.

McKay reappeared, freshly shaved and dressed, rifling through his suitcase. Spence sat up slowly.

"Hey, Mick?"

"Yeah?"

"You don't think Grace pulled back because things got too... friendly?"

"How do you mean?"

"I mean, when she got here, she told me she was just planning to relax and read a stack of books. Then she met Megs. Then me. Now she's hanging out with the whole group. You think she's overwhelmed? Or... maybe people have been bugging her about relationships and she's over it?"

McKay considered that. "Could be. Girls talk about that stuff a lot, don't they?"

"She told me her friends and family are always trying to set her up. Church people too. I can relate. I swear, as soon as someone hears you're divorced, they think you need to be fixed up immediately."

That last sentence came out bitter, but Spence didn't regret it.

McKay quieted. "Cuz... I'm sorry."

Spence waved it off. "No, it's fine. I know you meant well, pushing me to come. And honestly? I'm glad you did. But maybe for Grace, it's different. If everyone's pressuring her and now she's seeing couples start to form here, maybe it's just too much."

"Yeah. Katie was really shaken up after the zip line, but I wouldn't be surprised if they talked about more than that."

"She told me once that her ex had an affair. I can't even imagine."

"I know. And I don't want to know. Julie leaving was hard enough. I don't think I could handle that kind of betrayal."

They were both quiet for a beat too long before McKay stood and tossed his towel into the bathroom.

"Hey, Spence?"

"Yeah?"

"What do you think about Megs?"

Spence smiled knowingly. "How did I know that was coming?"

McKay chuckled, then rubbed his face. "I can't help it. The last couple days with her have been... fun. Really fun. Is it crazy to think about something more?"

Spence raised an eyebrow. "Depends. What's 'something more'? You asking her to dance? Spend tomorrow together?"

McKay shook his head. "No. I mean... I think I want to ask her to keep in touch after the cruise. Maybe come visit?"

"Is that all?"

McKay looked up through his fingers. "Maybe not."

Spence blinked. He'd never seen McKay like this. Normally, his cousin was the human version of a revolving door when it came to relationships.

"What exactly are you thinking?"

McKay sat down at the desk, elbows resting on the wood. He looked serious—genuinely thoughtful.

"I don't know. I've just... never felt like this. It's different."

Spence almost teased him. Awww, you're growing up. But instead, he just nodded. "Look, you don't have to decide anything right now. But if it feels right? Go with it. Just take it one day at a time."

McKay cracked a grin. "I can handle that."

Spence smiled. "Besides, you've already got the perfect opening line."

"Oh yeah?"

"'Hey Megs, I once outran a guy with a machete in Chile. You in?'"

McKay laughed. "Hey, that might actually work."

Chapter 66

Grace stood outside the restaurant a moment longer than she meant to. The others were gathered just inside, talking and laughing while they waited for a table, but she couldn't quite make her feet move.

She needed a pause. A breath. Something to hold on to before stepping into the swirl of togetherness again.

Her eyes flicked toward the glass doors. Spence stood near Missy, laughing at something McKay said. They looked... comfortable. Familiar. Like maybe something had shifted when she wasn't looking. That possibility sat like a stone in her stomach.

The compliments about her photos still echoed in her mind, and she didn't doubt their sincerity. But all of it— Missy's easy charm, Spence's warmth, the way everyone just seemed to click—left Grace feeling like an extra puzzle piece. One that didn't quite belong.

She hadn't expected this. She came for sun, for solitude. Maybe a few polite chats and the chance to take some great photos. Not to get attached. Not to start hoping.

And certainly not to feel the sharp twinge of jealousy.

"Grace, there you are!" Megs bounced out and linked her arm through hers, all sunshine and sequins. "We're just waiting on the table. Come stand with us."

Grace let herself be tugged inside. She plastered on a smile, unsure if it looked natural or brittle.

Inside, Missy waved her over while Katie made room. Spence stood just behind them. He glanced over when she joined and gave her that easy, open smile.

She didn't quite know how to return it.

"We were just talking about you," Missy said with a grin. "In a good way, I promise."

"Oh yeah?" Grace said carefully, trying to find solid ground.

"They're trying to convince me to bribe you for more pictures," Spence added.

Grace managed a half-laugh. "No bribery needed. I think I might actually enter a couple of the contest ones. Missy and Katie helped me pick a few."

"You should," he said, and it was the sincerity in his voice that nearly undid her. "They're incredible. You've got something special."

The knot in her chest eased just a little, the warmth of his words working its way in like light through a crack in the blinds.

But still, she couldn't stop wondering—what if she was misreading everything?

Megs leaned in, eyes wide. "I still say the Charlie's Angels one needs to be printed on a tote bag."

Grace laughed, despite herself. "Only if we all get one."

"Done!" Missy declared.

The host called their group, and they began to gather their things. As they moved toward the table, Grace caught Spence looking at her again. She felt her breath hitch.

He was still watching her.

And for just a moment, it felt like maybe she hadn't been forgotten after all.

Chapter 67

By the time Grace slid into her seat at the table, the sound of friendly chatter had settled into a comfortable hum. The server took their drink orders while Megs and McKay cracked jokes about who ate the most at the buffet yesterday.

Grace smiled, but her fingers fidgeted with the edge of her napkin.

She was trying to act normal, like everything felt fine. Like her stomach wasn't still twisted up in knots from earlier. Like she hadn't spent the better part of the afternoon convincing herself she wasn't being edged out by a connection she could see forming between Missy and Spence.

She'd told herself not to care. That she didn't come here looking for a love story.

But feelings didn't ask for permission. They just happened.

Spence sat across from her, laughing at something Katie said, his arms folded on the table, relaxed and casual in a way that made her ache. He hadn't done anything wrong. If anything, he'd been kind. Warm. Present.

And maybe that was the problem.

"Hey Grace?" Missy nudged her with a grin. "You OK over there? You got quiet."

Grace blinked out of her thoughts and offered a small smile. "Yeah, I'm good. Just soaking it all in."

Spence glanced her way at that, his brow lifting just a little. His gaze lingered a moment longer than it needed to, as if he were trying to read her.

She looked down at her water glass, then forced herself to speak up. "Katie, I meant to ask—did you still want a copy of that photo with you and Spence at the temple?"

Katie lit up. "Yes! Oh, can you email it to me? I want to use it in my end-of-year blog recap."

"I still can't believe how many good ones it looked like you got," Katie said as she looked over the menu. "I thought maybe two or three would turn out okay, but I was wrong from what you showed us on the camera screen."

Grace shrugged, trying not to overthink it. "Some were luck. Some were angle. And I had Spence's fancy camera."

"You also had the eye," Missy added. "That's not equipment. That's talent."

Spence smiled, clearly pleased. "Still think your pyramid shot is the best one. That one with the sunrise glow?"

"Oh that one was amazing!" Megs chimed in. "Total contest-winner vibes. Like, if that's not in National Geographic, I don't even know."

Grace glanced down, a little overwhelmed by how much faith they had in her.

"I've never entered a real photo contest before," she admitted. "But I guess... why not? If it doesn't place, at least I'll have some great prints."

"Well, we're all rooting for you," McKay said, sipping his water. "And if you do win? We expect a celebratory dinner. With desserts. Fancy ones."

"Oh, is that what's in it for you?" Grace laughed.

"Obviously," he deadpanned. "We're a highly motivated support group."

Conversation flowed from there, and Grace let herself be pulled along with it.

Maybe she hadn't completely imagined the connection between her and Spence. Maybe it was real. But even if it wasn't—these people, this laughter, this moment—it was still something she was grateful to be part of.

For tonight, that was enough.

Chapter 68

The waiter arrived with a large tray piled high with steaming plates, the scent of garlic and grilled meat curling through the air like a promise. As dishes were handed out one by one, Spence opened his linen napkin and draped it across his lap, trying not to think too much about the fact that Grace hadn't said more than a sentence to him all evening.

The waiter leaned in to serve Megs when someone passing behind him jostled him off balance. He stumbled—just enough to bump the back of Missy's chair. Missy jerked forward, startled, her hand flying out to steady herself. It landed squarely on Spence's thigh.

Spence froze mid-motion. His fork clinked against the plate. Missy gasped as her own fork skittered to the floor.

"Sorry! Sorry!" she said quickly, already ducking under the table.

Spence leaned down too, his hand instinctively going for the fallen utensil. Their heads collided with a soft thud.

"Ow—sorry!"

"No, my fault!"

He managed to snag the fork first, lifting it just as the flustered waiter apologized and rushed away to get a clean one.

Spence set the fork by his glass of Sprite and noticed Missy's hand was still resting on his leg.

"Oh—uh..." He gently shifted, hoping to dislodge her without calling attention to it.

Too late. A half-second glance around the table told him everyone had seen it.

McKay's eyebrow arched high enough to hit orbit, and even Megs looked like she was trying not to smirk. Spence cleared his throat and focused hard on his hamburger, now suspiciously less appetizing.

"Here," he said, nudging the fork toward Missy. "Take mine. I'll use the new one when it gets here."

"Are you sure?"

"Yeah. I'm not in a hurry." He offered a half-smile.

She smiled back and took the fork with a soft "Thanks."

Conversation slowly picked back up as the group eased past the awkward moment. Spence caught snippets of McKay and Megs chatting across the table, Katie laughing at something Missy had said, but he felt oddly disconnected from it all.

"Um, I'm really sorry," Missy murmured beside him.

Spence shook his head. "Why? The waiter bumped into you."

Still, he leaned toward her and lowered his voice. "I just didn't mean to—you know..."

Missy waved it off. "Seriously. It's fine. Just forget it. And thanks for the fork."

He nodded and shifted back, trying to realign his focus. The burger on his plate still looked excellent, but something about the moment made everything taste a little off.

He kept sneaking glances at Grace. She hadn't laughed with him tonight the way she had before. In fact, she hadn't looked at him much at all. And when she finally did turn slightly in his direction, it was only to speak to Megs and McKay, her back still partially to him.

He sighed and leaned back in his chair.

He had planned to talk to her tonight. Not in front of the group—just her. He needed to get things off his chest before it drove him insane. The last few days had stirred up more emotion than he was prepared for. But now that he'd finally admitted to himself that there might be something—and that he wanted to explore it—Grace seemed further away than ever.

Spence picked up a fry, chewed absently, and waited for the right moment.

But the moment never came.

Chapter 69

After dinner, the group had agreed to meet up in Spence and McKay's room before heading out to play shuffleboard. Grace tagged along only because it seemed expected. The others were all in the process of gathering, buzzing with excitement over the photos they'd taken earlier that day. Grace didn't want to deal with any of it—not the pictures, not the game, and especially not the growing ache in her chest.

All she could think about was Missy's hand on Spence's leg and how long they'd been under the table together at dinner. The image replayed in her mind like an unwelcome highlight reel. It felt like confirmation of something she hadn't wanted to believe: that maybe she was the odd one out. Again.

The two of them really did fit. She could see it now. The smiles. The easy camaraderie. She told herself she should be happy for them—shouldn't she be?

Still, she tried to bow out of both the game and the photo gathering, but Megs would hear none of it. "Come on! These are going to be epic. We're immortalized in our own ridiculous action movie posters!"

Grace had to force a smile, but Megs had already bounced away.

Grace clutched her camera as she approached Spence and McKay's cabin. Her stomach flipped with dread. What if the other girls weren't there yet? What if it was just the two guys? What if it was just Spence?

Her hand raised to knock on the door, and her mind spiraled. She wasn't sure she could handle watching McKay and Megs flirt their way through another conversation. And she certainly wasn't ready to sit beside Spence while Missy leaned in, sharing inside jokes and fork accidents.

Why had she even come?

Before she could decide to walk away, the door swung open.

"Hey, you're the first ones here," Spence said, a little surprised. "Come on in."

Grace swallowed hard. Exactly what she feared. Just her and Megs. She could have made up a reason to be late—said she needed more batteries or got lost on the wrong deck. Something.

She followed Megs inside, keeping her head down. She found the nearest chair and slid into it, clutching the stack of printed photos like a lifeline.

McKay and Megs started chatting immediately, their conversation bubbling with ease and laughter. It was as if no time had passed between them, like they shared some secret current that everyone else was just meant to observe from the sidelines.

Grace glanced up and found Spence watching her.

She dropped her gaze and pretended to focus on sorting the photographs. Her fingers fumbled with the edges of the glossy prints, rearranging them for the sake of having something to do—anything that didn't require meeting his eyes.

"Hey," McKay said suddenly, standing by the door with an ice bucket in hand. "We're gonna grab some ice. We'll be back in like five minutes, OK?"

"Yeah, great," Grace said, trying to keep her tone neutral.

McKay and Megs ducked out of the room. Grace knew the ice machine was just a few doors down. That didn't give her much time. But the door clicked shut behind them, leaving only the quiet hum of the air conditioning and Spence.

Her stomach clenched.

She pretended to be absorbed in the photos again, but she could feel him getting closer.

"Grace," Spence said, his voice lower now, more serious. "Can we talk?"

She nodded but didn't look up. She flipped to another photo. Then another.

"I mean it," he said, gently placing his hands over hers to stop the movement. "I need to talk to you."

Her heart sank. Here it comes. The speech. The "I really like you, but..." followed by the slow unraveling of the trip's best memories.

She braced herself and looked him in the eyes.

"OK," she said, trying to sound composed.

Spence hesitated, studying her. Grace felt like she was staring down a cliff edge and had just been told to jump. She steeled herself for whatever was coming next.

She just hoped she'd be able to smile when it was over.

Chapter 70

Grace couldn't believe she was alone in a room with Spence. She glanced toward the door, wishing Megs and McKay would hurry up with that ice bucket. But the hallway was quiet, and she was alone with the one person she didn't know how to talk to anymore.

Spence opened his mouth once, then closed it. He shifted in his seat and rubbed his palms on his jeans, the way someone might before giving a speech they didn't want to mess up. His confidence—the kind she'd seen so clearly when he teased McKay or zipped across the rainforest—seemed to vanish, replaced by something unsure and vulnerable.

He took a breath.

"I'm really nervous right now," he said, voice low. "I don't know why this is so hard, but it is. Maybe because it matters."

Grace's fingers curled together in her lap. The pounding in her chest had nothing to do with fear of zip lines or ancient heights. "You don't have to be nervous," she offered, even though her own throat was tight.

"Yeah," he said. "I kind of do."

He reached over, gently stilling her hands. "Grace, I need to say something. And I need you to really hear me, because I think there's been a lot of mixed signals, and I don't want to mess this up."

The quiet between them was thick. This wasn't the kind of silence that begged to be filled with chatter—it was the kind that asked for courage.

Then he continued, with a mixture of steadiness and fear, "I noticed you were upset today, and I've been trying to figure out what I did. Because I want to fix it. Because I care."

This was it. She braced herself for what she thought would come next: the "you're great, but..." speech. She'd heard it before. It always ended the same way.

"OK," she whispered, finally looking up.

Spence studied her face. Did he have any idea what he'd meant to her this week? Probably not. She doubted she even meant much to him, not really. Maybe just someone to talk to on a cruise ship.

"I'm so sorry," he began. "I don't know what I did—"

"No, it's OK," she interrupted. "I get it."

His brow furrowed. "You get what?"

"That we only just met. And it was nice. It was fun. But I understand."

"You understand what?" he asked again, slower this time.

"That you're just not interested," she said, her voice cracking. She folded her hands in her lap and stared at the floor. Her chest felt tight, like her ribs were made of glass and one wrong breath would shatter her completely.

"What are you talking about, Grace?"

"I mean, we had a good time. But we don't really know each other. And it's not like we live anywhere close, and I have a kid, and... It's OK, Spence. Really. I get that you want to hang out with Missy or whatever, and I promise I won't make it awkward."

He blinked at her. "Grace. That's not what I was going to say."

Her breath caught. "It's...not?"

"No." He rubbed the back of his neck. "I was going to say that I noticed you seemed off today. I thought maybe I did something to upset you. I've been wracking my brain trying to figure it out, and I wanted to apologize if it was something I said or did."

Her head spun. "You were...worried about me?"

"Of course I was. I care about you. And I just—I didn't know how to bring it up without sounding dumb."

Grace blinked back a sudden wave of tears. "You...care about me?"

Spence stood up and paced for a second. "Why is this so hard?" he muttered, then turned back toward her. "Look, I didn't plan on this. I didn't come on this cruise looking to connect with someone. But then there you were, talking about photography and history and finding meaning in these ruins. You made me feel like myself again."

She watched him, stunned.

"I don't know what happens after this cruise," he continued. "Maybe we'll just be friends. Maybe not. But I don't want it to end here without saying something. Grace Jensen, I'd really like to get to know you better. Not just for a cruise, but for real."

A thousand thoughts flooded her at once: Aaron, her job, North Carolina, the unlikelihood of ever seeing him again after this week.

But louder than all of that was the thrum of her heart, the one that had been trying to speak up for days now.

"You...don't want this to end?" she asked, tentative.

"No," he said softly. "I really don't."

She swallowed hard. "Even if I'm a single mom who overthinks everything?"

He smiled, gently. "Especially then."

"Spence, no..."

The words were barely out of her mouth before Grace regretted how they sounded. Not what she meant—not really. Not no as in rejection. Just... no, this isn't what I expected. No, I'm terrified.

Spence leaned back slightly, as if bracing himself.

"Oh," he said quietly. The hurt that flashed across his face made her stomach twist.

"No," she repeated, softer this time. "I don't mean no, like... no. I mean... this is all just really unexpected. And I don't know what to do with it."

Spence let out a breath he'd clearly been holding. His posture softened but his eyes searched hers, still unsure. "So... not no?"

"Just..." Grace took a shaky breath. Spence caught her by surprise. She was torn between fear... and hope. She didn't know what to do with that.

His eyes softened. He opened his mouth like he was about to say something—something that would tip the scale one way or the other—but before the words could come out, the door handle jiggled.

Voices carried through the hall as McKay and Megs returned, laughing loudly about something involving a soda machine and a rogue ice cube.

Spence gave a little sigh and scooted back to the edge of the bed, the moment suspended like a crystal mid-drop. Neither of them spoke as the door opened.

Chapter 71

Spence knew it was a long shot, but it still crushed him when she said no. And of course, that was the exact moment McKay and Megs returned to the suite. He didn't know what Grace had meant to say after that no—but whatever it was, it was lost now.

He tried not to let the hurt show. If only he'd been more articulate. Maybe then she wouldn't have looked so stricken. Maybe then she would've finished her sentence.

"Hey, guys, look who we met in the hall." McKay's voice was bright as he hoisted the bucket of ice. Spence glanced over his shoulder and saw not only Megs, but also Missy and Katie.

He stood awkwardly, then settled into the chair beside Grace. She still hadn't moved. Her mouth was slightly open, like she'd frozen mid-thought the second the door opened.

The group filtered into the room, but Spence couldn't stop watching her. She looked pale. Fragile. Like she might cry. The last thing he wanted was to upset her.

Panic sparked. Was this why she'd seemed so distant all day? Had she known he was starting to care and wanted to spare him the pain of being led on? Maybe that's what all the space was about. Maybe this was her kind way of letting him down.

But what had all that been about Missy?

Missy was nice, sure. But she wasn't Grace.

Whatever memories they were making as a group—playing games, taking pictures, zip-lining—it was the time with Grace he knew he'd carry with him. The rest would fade. But Grace would stay clear.

She'd stay alive in his mind.

Forever.

The word came out of nowhere. Forever? Who thinks about forever with someone they've only known a few days?

And yet—he didn't hate the thought.

In fact, it warmed something deep inside of him.

Grace... forever.

It sounded ridiculous. And it was ridiculous. But it didn't feel ridiculous. It felt right.

If he weren't completely insane, he'd stand up and tell her right now. Just lay it all out. But how exactly do you slip forever into a conversation with someone who barely knows you?

No. That was crazy.

Still, he looked at her, aching to know what she'd meant to say. Wishing the words hadn't been interrupted. Knowing he might never get that moment back.

Because once the group dove into the pictures, and then headed to shuffleboard, that window would close.

And he wasn't sure he'd be brave enough to open it again.

Chapter 72

They were waiting to play shuffleboard, and thanks to McKay, Spence and Grace had ended up paired together. No one seemed surprised when McKay picked Megs for his team. That left roommates Missy and Katie to bring up the rear.

The pairing would have suited Spence just fine—if not for Grace's no still echoing in his head. It hung between them like storm clouds in paradise. She didn't seem as easygoing as when they first met, and he couldn't shake the feeling that he'd blown it.

Blown it big time.

How do you go from never wanting to risk your heart again... to thinking about forever with someone you just met?

He must've been nuts. Or maybe it was just the atmosphere. Singles Cruise logic. Everything on this ship was a little skewed. Maybe the ocean air rewired people's brains – his brains.

Still, he should've known better. A woman with a child had way more on the line than he did. When his heart broke, it was just his. She'd be risking two.

He shook his head, trying to clear the spiral of thoughts. Hoping shuffleboard would somehow help him win back a moment that had already slipped away.

"What's wrong, Spence?" Missy leaned closer to be heard over the crowd gathering near the shuffleboard court.

"Oh, nothing. Just... thinking." His voice came out softer than he meant it to.

"Are you sure?"

He rolled his shoulders and offered a lopsided smile. "You know how it goes. Standing here makes me realize how much we've packed into the last three days."

"I hear that." She stretched her arms over her head. "I hope they call us soon."

When their names were finally called, it was clear none of them really remembered how the game worked. The court was long, with triangle markings at either end and round discs—biscuits—stacked at the ready. Spence grabbed one of the long sticks and squinted at it. "This thing's called a cue, right? Looks like something you'd use to poke a gator."

Grace laughed, and he relaxed a little.

The rules were a mystery, but everyone decided to just go for it and hope they didn't end up in the -10 zone. Or off the court entirely.

"Okay, here goes nothing," Grace said, lining up a yellow disc. She leaned forward, wobbled slightly, and sent it sliding. The biscuit wavered, then landed squarely in the 8-point zone.

"Yes! I got an eight! Top that!" She raised the cue in the air like a sword. "That's the best I've gotten all night!"

"Way to rub it in, Grace. But you are going down. I'm aiming for the ten this time!"

"Just make sure it's not the kitchen again."

"Hey, I meant to land in the -10. Adds drama."

"And then three more times in a row?"

"What can I say? It's a gift!"

She snorted. "Your go. Try not to sabotage us again."

Spence lined up the disc and gave it a nudge with the cue. It coasted across the court, wobbled at the edge of the scoring zone, and just—barely—nudged into the 10-point tip.

He threw his arms in the air. "Go, go, go—YES!" Then turned to Grace and did a ridiculous little shuffle victory dance. "Boom! That's how it's done."

"You think you're all that just because you got ten points?"

"You know it. That's the right ten this time, thank you very much. Whatcha gonna do now, wise guy?"

He walked over to her, daring her to answer, and that's when it happened.

She looked at him through her lashes, eyes glinting with laughter and something more. Time froze as the light caught her just right and something between them pulsed.

And he kissed her.

He didn't think.

He just kissed her.

It was bold. Wild. Possibly the most daring thing he'd done all year—maybe ever.

But in that kiss, he realized what he'd been missing.

He wasn't just missing connection.

He was missing her.

She was everything he hadn't known he still wanted.

Grace.

As they parted, breathless, he knew he needed to explain himself. "Grace, I..."

"No," she interrupted softly. "Let me. Let me finish what I should've finished before."

He didn't get a chance to ask what she meant.

Because she kissed him again.

This time she started it—and it was even sweeter than before.

When they finally pulled away, the sound of clapping reminded them they weren't alone.

Their friends were watching, cheering.

Grace turned a deep, crimson red—possibly the most beautiful shade Spence had ever seen. He doubted he'd ever get tired of seeing that.

"About darn time, cuz!" McKay called, grinning as he slung an arm around Megs.

Megs elbowed him. "He's not the only slow one in this bunch."

McKay stared at her, mock offended. "Slow? SLOW? No one's ever called me slow."

Megs grabbed his face, pulled him down, and kissed him quick on the lips. "Nope. You're slow, you lug."

Missy and Katie burst into giggles.

Spence didn't care. He looked at Grace—really looked at her.

Then he reached for her hand.

And she didn't let go.

Epilogue

Grace deplaned in Chile, the late afternoon sun warm against the glass windows of the airport. She'd worked hard to save for this trip and planned to make the most of it. Slinging her camera bag over one shoulder and her purse over the other, she made her way to baggage claim before heading through customs.

She could hardly believe she was here—let alone that she was here to photograph Megs and McKay's wedding. The only thing she didn't question was why they chose Chile. McKay had served his mission here, and it was so perfectly, delightfully Megs to want to marry at the Santiago Temple where her missionary-turned-fiancé once walked every day.

When it came time to pick a photographer, they'd immediately called Grace. She hadn't hesitated before saying yes. And they'd promised her full creative reign—not just temple photos on their wedding day, but a mountaintop shoot, wedding clothes and all.

She at least gave them the decency of waiting until the day after their wedding night. It was the least she could do.

It didn't take long to find her bags, and while waiting in the customs line, Grace let herself savor just how far she'd come in a few short months.

She'd entered that cruise photo contest on a whim—or more accurately, after much urging and outright threats from her new friends. And somehow, she'd won.

The cruise line loved the silly group picture taken among the ruins. Her local paper ran a feature about her just as she was packing for this trip. It was her fourth interview since the announcement.

Her boss at the camera shop used his contacts to get her a print display in local coffee shops and libraries. Soon, her phone wouldn't stop ringing. People fell in love with the joy in her group portraits—and the grandeur of her shots from Central America. Several travel agents commissioned posters. One client? Her ex-husband. He even paid for it.

Three months ago, she shot her first beach wedding in North Carolina. Then one in the Appalachian foothills. And just last week, a call came from San Antonio asking her to shoot a wedding next year at the Alamo.

She had future weddings lined up in Stonehenge. In Greece. In Egypt.

"State the nature of your business in Chile?" the customs officer asked in clipped Spanish-accented English.

Grace looked up from her suitcase. "I'm here for a wedding. I'm the photographer."

He eyed her carefully and motioned to the conveyor belt. "Anything to claim?"

"No."

"And this bag?"

She tightened her grip on her shoulder strap. "My camera. I'm shooting the wedding."

"How long will you be staying?"

"Just two weeks."

Two weeks she planned to enjoy—even if she was technically working. A travel magazine had asked her to do a photo essay, hoping she could recreate the magic of her Central American shoot. They'd even given her a modest expense account. It wasn't her first essay for them—but it felt like the most important.

"Photographing a wedding, huh?" the customs agent asked again, squinting. "You should enjoy yourself while you're here. Want a couple of good locations?"

Grace blinked. "Uh—sure!"

She'd planned to wing it, or maybe ask McKay for ideas. She'd spent the last few weeks buried in destination wedding blogs but still didn't know how to plan for a place she'd never been.

The man grew thoughtful. "There's plenty in Santiago. But you might like Cerro Santa Lucía. It's a classic. Charles Darwin stayed there once. Many couples get engaged there."

"Really? That sounds perfect."

He nodded. "Also... Teatro Municipal. Every major performance goes through there. And the art crowd here... they're colorful."

Before she could ask what that meant, he stamped her passport and handed it back.

"Welcome to Chile," he said. "Good luck with the photos. I hope you enjoy your stay."

Grace gathered her belongings and stepped toward the sliding doors that would lead her into Santiago. She paused, her heart full. A deep breath steadied her.

Was she ready for all the changes in her life?

Maybe. Maybe not.

But life had offered her something precious. A second chance. And she planned to take it.

She walked into the arrival hall, surrounded by the blur of people collecting bags and greeting family. Spanish swirled through the air in a mix of accents. The chaos was colorful, beautiful.

She set her bags down and reached for her camera. She didn't even look through the lens to check settings—just found that one perfect thing to capture.

She clicked the shutter.

Then she lowered the camera, smiling at her subject.

"It's about time you got here," Spence said, grin wide and eyes soft. "I've had to live two whole days without you. I nearly died."

"Oh, stop being dramatic, you nut. Aaron is safe with his grandparents, and the newspaper is off my back. I'm here now."

"I still can't believe we had to stop here before heading to Perth. I should shoot McKay for scheduling his wedding this week."

That was the last thing he said before sweeping her into his arms.

Grace looked into his eyes, heart thudding.

And melted into the kiss from her new husband.

Author's Note

Dear Reader, Life is a journey—and not always a smooth cruise.

Sometimes it's stormy. Sometimes it's shipwrecked. And sometimes... it's a surprise detour that leads you somewhere better than you imagined.

This book was born from one of those stormy seasons—and yes, it's definitely a detour from my usual genres.

Divorce—especially when faith is involved—can feel like spiritual whiplash.

You're not just grieving a relationship; you're questioning your worth, your identity, your direction.

I've been there. And I know how lonely and vast that ocean can feel, searching the horizon for a safe harbor with none in sight.

But here's what I believe with my whole heart:

You are not broken.

You are not less.

You are still made of stardust and grace.

You still have intrinsic worth.

No doctrine—real or imagined—can change that. Not in any faith.

This story leans heavily into LDS culture because that's the story that needed to be told.

I hope it reaches those within the wide LDS community who need a reminder that love after divorce is possible—and that faith, in all its forms, can be rebuilt.

But this story isn't just for one faith community.

It's for anyone who's had to rebuild, recover, or rediscover.

Anyone who's ever been blindsided by life and still dared to believe that healing—and love— might be possible.

Find what's here for your faith walk and hold onto it. Remember, it's our differing beliefs that build the rich tapestry of our world culture.

My own spiritual journey has been a winding one.

It's included a grounding in the mythologies of ancient cultures, three very different religious schools, a love of the natural rhythms of the world, and way more study than the average person.

I've never quite fit perfectly into any faith culture—but I've been grateful to be welcomed into many.

To my friends across all faith practices—and to those with none—I love you, and I'm thankful for your support.

Yes, this book is a romance. And a funny one, I hope.

But it's also a story about finding faith again—whether that means faith in yourself, in love, in life, or in something divine.

If you're wondering why this book is so different from my usual writing—this is why. It was purpose-driven. Personal.

Born out of a conversation with a friend going through her own stormy season... and so much more.

Sometimes, when a story asks to be written, you write it— even if it's not what people expect.

And don't get me wrong—after watching over a thousand Hallmark movies, I do love a good "sweet romance."

Religious romance just isn't my usual writing style. I prefer to write my stories with a bit more ~magic~.

That said, a wise person once said that today's magic is tomorrow's science—and I firmly believe that.

I also believe there's nothing more magical, in the best sense of the word, than talking about faith. Both faith and magic are born from the hope for things unseen and not yet understood.

After 50 years on this planet, I've seen yesterday's science fiction become today's science fact— and honestly? That's pretty magical, too.

If this book gave you even a flicker of joy, or helped you believe your best days might still be ahead...then this journey was worth it.

Thank you for coming aboard.

May your seas be a little calmer from here.

And if you like stories with magic, zombies, or space, maybe I'll see you on anther journey. If not, thanks for joining me on this trip.

—Jacalyn

Acknowledgments

This story wouldn't exist without the messy and magical process of healing—and the many souls who stood as lighthouses along the way.

To the countless people I've counseled, cried with, and prayed for—this book carries your stories. Grace and Spence might be fictional, but they're also pieces of each person that sat in the rubble of a life collapsing around them and dared to hope again. If you ever felt like your life began after everything fell apart, know you're not alone. This is for you.

To the friends I've walked alongside through addiction, divorce, and heartbreak—thank you for trusting me with your truth. You gave me the courage to speak mine and inspired me in so many ways. To my writing group: you championed this story when it was still a blurry sketch, asked thoughtful questions, and reminded me that love stories are for everyone. Your faith in the universal reach of this book kept me writing when I second guessed myself.

To the students, professors, and communities I encountered across multiple faith traditions as I've walked this path of life— thank you for expanding my spiritual vocabulary. Your wisdom helped shape a story that hopefully reaches beyond a single doctrine, while honoring the beauty of many.

To the historians and cultural scholars—both academic and amateur—who share their insights about Central America and its deep, sacred past: thank you for inspiring the tapestry that helped re-frame what faith might look like for a modern heart.

To the internet (yes, really)—for making it possible for me to deep dive through centuries of spiritual questions and archaeological wonders without ever changing out of pajamas while researching this book because I couldn't afford to take this fantasy cruise.

And finally, to every reader who's ever felt unlovable after loss:
You are not alone.
You are not too late.
You are not broken.
You are loved.
And your story still has more chapters.

More from Erendi Publishing

Juan of the Dead

Jacalyn Boggs

Giant Killer Bats of Alamogordo

By Jack Morse

Threshold

Various Authors

A Collection of Small Endings

JC Rock

If you enjoyed this book, consider leaving a review to help other readers find it!

About the Author

Jacalyn Boggs lives in Northern Virginia with her chihuahua, Nephi. She loves sunshine, the night sky, traveling the world, and dancing to the music only she hears. Raising two children taught her you never know what's around the next bend.

Always a dreamer, Jacalyn loves reading and watching movies. Her favorite fiction is that which explores the world in some new way. She's currently working on several other writing projects, including the next book in The Reanimated World Tour series.